Royal Bastards MC

Nashville, TN Chapter

USA Today Bestselling Author

MORGAN JANE MITCHELL

Copyright

Hallow's Eve, Royal Bastards MC: Nashville, TN Chapter © 2021 Morgan Jane Mitchell

Cover design © 2021 Morgan Jane Mitchell

www.morganjanemitchell.com

First Edition

ISBN: **9798491940035**

ROYAL BASTARDS CODE

PROTECT: The club and your brothers come before anything else, and must be protected at all costs. **CLUB** is **FAMILY**.

RESPECT: Earn it & Give it. Respect club law. Respect the patch. Respect your brothers. Disrespect a member and there will be hell to pay.

HONOR: Being patched in is an honor, not a right. Your colors are sacred, not to be left alone, and **NEVER** let them touch the ground.

OL' LADIES: Never disrespect a member's or brother's Ol'Lady. **PERIOD.**

CHURCH is **MANDATORY.**

LOYALTY: Takes precedence over all, including well-being.

HONESTY: Never **LIE, CHEAT,** or **STEAL** from another member or the club.

TERRITORY: You are to respect your brother's property and follow their Chapter's club rules.

TRUST: Years to earn it...seconds to lose it.

NEVER RIDE OFF: Brothers do not abandon their family.

Hallow's Eve
Royal Bastards MC:
Nashville, TN Chapter

If Eve knew the real Hallow, she'd run far away...

When Eve goes to work dressed as her namesake, she doesn't expect much excitement at the honky-tonk's annual Halloween party. A gang of bikers locking everyone in until they find a killer, now that's exciting. Believing she's merely part of a murder mystery dinner, Eve plays along by helping a gorgeous fallen angel find the killer.

Stumbling onto another dead body crashes her illusions.

Faced with real danger Eve falls into the strong arms of Hallow who's more like the fallen angel he's dressed as than she knows. Too bad his brothers decide to take her hostage as they leave the bar in pursuit of the killer.

A member of the Royal Bastards MC, Hallow is more than prepared to protect Eve on their wild night, but he isn't prepared to fall in love. Costume complete with apple or not, Eve's no temptress. She's as innocent as an angel. Hallow plans to snatch her from heaven, corrupt her and keep her for himself.

For all the songs that played in this novel visit
Hallow Eve's Playlist on Spotify

**Royal Bastards MC: Nashville, TN
Chapter
Reading Order/ Standalones**

Hallow's Eve (Hallow)

Royal Road (Kingpin)

TBA(Opry)

TBA(Riff)

TBA(Gunn)

TBA(Thorn)

TBA(Plague)

TBA(Levi)

CHAPTER 1

EVE

"Bridezillas over there." I informed Donette of the bachelorette party in the corner. Ever since she was left at the altar, my bestie couldn't handle the brides to be who stormed the honky-tonk highway.

Donette let her rage show for a second with a primal grunt right in my ear. "Better than the bikers around the stage," she retorted.

In the middle of Bootsies, not to be confused with the famous Tootsies, we hugged up like a couple. It was the only way for us to hear one another over the live bands. A cover of Hank Williams Jr.'s "Family Tradition" thundered, and the crowd sang along with their parts. It gave us a short break from slinging beer and Tennessee whisky.

"Trade me, okay?" Donette gave up the bikers for the brides. "You can handle bikers."

I ignored her comment about me. "Are you sure?" "Yes," she breathed in my ear. "I'm so over Dylan."

Silent, I nodded. It was her loss. Those girls were about to blow chunks. In their pink matching cowboy hats, they were drunk before they stepped off the pedal tavern they took here. Bikers on the other hand tipped well. Donette and I separated, crossed paths, and I headed to the stage. She hadn't been kidding. A huge pack of motorcycle men surrounded our fourth act. With their leather and chains, they stood out in the crowd of hillbilly hipsters.

An ice-cold hand landed on my shoulder. Whipping my head around, I glared at our head bartender, Ford. He bent down. Ford's lips grazed my ear. "Eve, don't bother. Let them come to the bar."

"What? Are they good tippers? You want my tips, Ford?" I practically shouted.

"Those guys are the Royal Bastards. Real assholes. I wish Grady would kick them out."

Rolling my eyes, I shrugged Ford's hand off me. My boss had never kicked out bikers before.

"I'm warning you, Eve. Don't get too close," Ford snapped as I walked away.

Get too close? That was practically my job. Nightly, I had to weave through the crowd of partygoers to take folks their drink orders. I'd been rubbing booties with people all night. Hell, I popped up between a couple kissing earlier. They were happy to get their shots of Jack Daniels, and I was

happy to shove their dollars in my pockets. Besides, Ford and his bartenders freaked if we barmaids didn't keep everyone from crowding his bar where they also served the only dish we made, Nashville Hot Chicken.

Preparing myself, I tied my grey Jack Daniels t-shirt up a bit higher and yanked the cuffs of my daisy dukes down a hair, so they didn't crawl up my ass again. I dove in. Swimming through the bikers, their beards tickled me as they bent to tell me their orders. Soon I was in front of my boss, Grady asking him to basically empty out a bottle of George Dickel.

"Why don't you just take the bottle and some glasses?"

"Great idea."

Balancing a slew of shot glasses in one hand and the bottle in the other, I waded into the crowd again. In a sea of roughnecks, I poured more than a dozen double shots of whiskey and filled my apron with cash. Sure, my ass got pinched by a few bikers, the men and one woman, but I turned to leave feeling pretty pleased. That was before I bumped face first into a stray biker. He grabbed a hold of my shoulders to steady me.

Towering over me, he opened his mouth to talk, but a wild woman materialized at his side. His lips shut tight. A biker bitch in head-to-toe leather, huge hoop earrings with spiky fuchsia hair snarled at me. Everything she had was out on the showroom floor as her tits were about ready to pop out and slap me. She raised her glass fixing to drown me in her drink.

Flinching, I squeezed my eyes shut, waiting to be doused in whiskey.

"Steph," the biker barked at her over the music. His grip on me disappeared.

As soon as his hands left my shoulders, I crumbled to the floor to dodge the splash. Luckily, Steph tossed her drink at him, not me. But Lordalmighty, her glass crashed onto the wooden floor, shattering beside me. Scared the dickens out of me. I screeched, not that anyone could hear me. Steph lunged at me. Other biker bitches had rushed over to hold her back just in time. Regardless, she snipped at him like an angry dog. I watched their mouths argue from my seat on the floor but couldn't make out a word over a country cover of some Bee Gees' song complete with falsetto. Apparently, the seventies were all the rage now. I blamed the popularity of beards.

Speaking of beards, to my surprise, the biker's focus turned to me as he offered his hand. Just to avoid the broken glass, I took it and let him haul me to my feet. At the sight of his dripping face, I automatically handed him the towel hanging off my apron. After all, that was my job. When he didn't take it, I dabbed his wet cheek and chest myself. Standing, I could hear the bitch now.

Her voice came like ice. "Tell me. This your whore now?"

"What's it to you?" he yelled, seized my waist and drew me to him.

I held my hands out to stop the man from carting me into a full embrace. Stepping away from his control, I squawked as loud as I could, "Excuse me, but I'm not a whore. And I don't dare date nasty bikers like you." I gave him a once over while I said it and noticed he was drop dead gorgeous. Still, I jutted my chin out with attitude.

And you could hear a pin drop.

It just so happened my exclamation corresponded with the very second the music stopped. It was as if the whole crowd stirred to stare at me. In the spotlight, my face reddened. My chest felt tight. The biker's mouth hung open. Steph laughed like a loon. Just as quick, the music resumed as a fiddle wailed. Overly embarrassed, I jetted back to the bar.

Ford was waiting for me. He leaned over. "You alright?"

Picking glass out of my hair, I bobbed my head. Now that everyone wasn't staring at me, I felt okay. Realizing he'd witnessed that awful scene but didn't come to my rescue, I plastered on a fake smile. "Just peachy," I said in a normal tone, not caring if he heard me.

The other bartenders, Jasper, Greta and Viv joined Ford to stare at me. Then Celie came over and tackled me, hugged me to her. Twice my age, my supervisor had been working here for ages. She trained all us girls and guys to grow thick skin but wasn't above lifting our chins when things got rough. I relaxed against her for a moment, taking the comfort she offered. Sucking in a breath, I smelled nothing but her heavy perfume. Oddly enough, she reminded me of my late mother, petite and thin, like me. However, where Celie was dark, I was pale with blonde hair. She had big blue eyes that stood out against her black hair, and I had brown eyes that blended in with my artificial lowlights. When she first met me, she said I was whiter than a frog's belly. In the wintertime I was but right now I had a bit of a tan.

After Celie came Grady, her ex and our big boss, under the rarely seen owners. Sexier than socks on a rooster, he just stood there, arms crossed, shaking his head.

"I'm fine, for real," I mouthed as I took off to find Donette to tell her what had happened.

For the rest of the evening, I avoided the bikers like the plague. The biker bitch had high tailed it out of here after my boss approached her. The guy, however, stuck around, but I refused to even look his way. I avoided him by stealing away to the breakroom as often as I could. Donette found me. We talked about tomorrow night which was Halloween when we'd be required to dress up. My bestie

would be coming as Lydia Deetz from *Beetlejuice*. I figured it was because she already looked like that actress, everyone said so. She claimed some guy always came as Beetlejuice but always came alone.

"There's a guy who always comes as Beetlejuice?"

"Not the same guy. Somebody different every year dresses as Beetlejuice. You can bet your bottom dollar, but you never see Lydia."

"Oh, gotcha." Donette was hoping tomorrow's Beetlejuice was hot underneath the makeup. I pictured Beetlejuice in my head and grimaced. "You're in search of someone who'd dress as Beetlejuice?"

"That's my type. I want a gothy geek like me. An Omega male."

"What's that?"

"Basically, the opposite of an Alpha male. I've had plenty of those. Men like my ex, Dylan." At the mention of her ex-fiancé, we had our usual moment of silence as she took a deep breath. When she recovered, she explained, "I'm looking for an Omega male to settle down with, become an Alpha mom." Donette was only two years older than me but was dying to get married and start a family. Since her ex-fiancé left her, I figured she'd been through every type of guy. But I wasn't one to judge.

"I've not even thought about it," I said, speaking of my costume though she hadn't asked. Also, I hadn't thought about what type of guy I liked. Donette and I didn't have to be polite to one another and ask questions. We just told each other what we wanted to and that was that. Simple. That was why Donette was my best friend in Nashville. We were easy. I liked easy. More than that, I was horrible at being polite and making conversations happen.

Eventually business wound down, and Grady handed me my Gibson acoustic guitar like always. "It's closing time, Eve."

As always, my eager smile thanked him. I was mighty grateful for the opportunity and that it was indeed closing time. Our last gig had just packed up. The five of them counted their tips at the bar. The lead singer, Ray tipped his Stetson and winked as I walked by. His eyes followed me as I stepped up onto the stage, but frowning, he shook his head. Yeah, he knew about me.

Grady set out the big glass tip jar, now empty, for me as I stood in front of our vintage style microphone. Looking out over the Thursday night stragglers, I reminded myself it was Friday morning. That the dozen or so folks left were all too drunk to notice me. As usual, I glanced around out over the long room, searching for someone to sing to. Portraits of so many stars who started their careers here on Lower Broad hung above the bar. Willie, black and white, in his Grand Ole Opry days tempted me, but my eyes locked

with the flat painted ones of our mechanical bull. Taco had been out of order for months. This one was for him. I hoped he liked Lyle Lovett. But moreover, I knew Grady would get a kick out of it. After all, he was the one who hired the bands.

As I sang "Closing Time", I changed up the lyrics. "Grady's been mixing drinks all evening... I know that man ain't right.... Celie's always giggling..."

Celie's laugh sounded, making my eyes travel to her as she flipped on the overhead lights. The neon glow disappeared to reveal a dirty bar. Squinting, I glanced around with a bit more confidence. As I strummed and got into a rhythm, I noticed folks doing just what I was singing. Ford arranged chairs and Donette loaded empty beer bottles onto the bar. The last band was still counting their money and Grady was sending folk's home. As more people left, I sang even better. My whole body relaxed as my bundle of nerves unwound. A real smile overtook my features as I belted out the last part of the song. I spied the biker from earlier exiting the building, Grady holding the door for him. My smile widened. When I sang the last notes, the place had cleared.

The singer in his Stetson stood and clapped first. He was joined by the rest of his band and our crew that was left. Blushing, I bowed a little before leaving the stage. I had a floor to mop.

"Where's Donette," I asked Grady when I was fixing to leave. We always walked to the parking garage together.

"She said to tell you, Goodnight, Irene."

I crossed my arms. "Again?" That was our code to let each other know we were leaving with a guy. I'd never gotten to use it. Meanwhile, Donette had done worn it out.

"Don't worry. Ford can walk you."

I didn't let my discomfort show on my face. "What about Celie?"

"She's already gone. Greta and Viv, too."

"The other girls?" I asked but knew only a few of the newbies, Donette and I had been closing. It was horrible, but I barely knew the new girls' names. Turnover was that high.

"Sent Shandra and Tinessa home before close. If you can wait for me, I'll walk you myself." Grady smirked and got a funny look in his eye. "Maybe we can get some coffee."

My nerves prickled, winding back up again. Grady had his eye on me, I knew, but he was more than twice my age, even older than his ex-wife Celie. Sure, he was a silver fox, but I didn't have enough fingers and toes to count all the reasons I shouldn't have coffee with him. For one thing, he had a set of twins in high school. "Oh, I've got to be on

my way home. I'm worn out." I yawned and stretched for good measure. "I'll find Ford."

"Titan up!" a man hollered from the second floor of the honky-tonk next door as Ford and I stepped out of Bootsies. I rolled my eyes as Ford echoed him. He was wearing his Tennessee Titan's jersey. Ford might pass for a kicker, but he was no football player. Just a rabid fan. There was likely some big win tonight that I knew nothing about. I'd never been big on sports.

"It's good you're having me walk you with those bikers out and about," Ford said right off.

"I'm more worried about the homeless trying to rob me," I muttered. There was a wad of cash in mainly ones shoved into my purse. Most of the time the vagrants on these streets were harmless, but at three a.m. with such easy pickings, a girl had to be careful.

"Weren't you the one?" Ford started to ask a question I got all too often.

"Yes, I'm the one. I kicked old man Henry in the groin. I thought he was going to attack me." Henry had been shining shoes on Broadway here in Nashville for nearly forty years. It happened when I was new. How was I to know the old man approaching me so quickly this early in the morning wasn't trying anything? Come to find out, Henry was only trying to give me something I dropped when I passed him. I don't even remember what but hauling off and kicking that sweet old man in his nutsack, I'd never live it down.

Ford laughed for a good while as we passed the other honky-tonks. They were all bigger than Bootsies with their multiple floors and rooftop bars. But at night, they were all the same. Dark inside and silent. You could hear a pin drop if Ford quit laughing. His chuckles echoed on the noiseless street. A chill ran over me, and I rubbed my arms to settle it. I glanced up to see the Batman building hovering over Broadway, lit up as always. That gave me some comfort. Usually, Donette and I would be rehashing the evening. Ford was full of questions since we didn't know each other well.

"You're from Alabama?"

"Arkansas," I answered and paused for a good while before I realized I should ask him where he was from. "You?"

"Volunteer, born and raised. You're here to play music. Hit it big, right?"

"Something like that." I didn't know Ford well enough to tell him I wasn't all I thought I'd be here in Nashville. That I could sing like an angel in the choir back home, actually in the choir of the Flipping First Baptist Church but froze on stage under the bright neon lights. "I make way more money serving nights than I would playing a morning gig." I shrugged. It was a truer fact than any. And

a morning gig would be all I could hope for if I could manage it. As it was, I'd given up even finding a band to play with until I got over my crippling nerves.

"Don't let the musicians fool you. They get base pay along with those tips."

"I know, but it ain't much." Some got as little as twenty-five dollars a day.

"Grady has to know you want to sing since he has you get up at closing time..."

Ford was on his way to finding out my secret. That I was too chicken shit to sing in front of a real crowd. Yeah, Grady knew all too well I couldn't sing in front of a big audience. We'd found that out my first week at Bootsies. That was why he let me sing at night when everyone had gone home. I needed to change the subject but blurted out, "I don't want to take advantage of Grady."

Ford caught onto that. "I thought Grady had a thing for you. Are you two...?"

"No way."

Ford fell silent. "You heard about tomorrow night?"

"The costume party?"

"Yeah, that but there's more. Some big surprise."

"What is it?"

"Don't know. Celie mentioned Grady had something big planned."

"Well." That in itself was surprising. Grady was nothing but consistent, and he's never had a surprise before.

"I'm thinking maybe it's an after party. Just for the employees, ya know?"

"That'd be nice since we won't really get to party tomorrow night on Halloween." Last year's Halloween was a letdown. I for one had been so eager to dress up but nothing exciting happened. Halloween had just been busier than a normal night which just meant I worked harder in clothes not meant for working.

"And since you and Grady aren't a thing, maybe you'll party with me?" Ford didn't miss a beat.

Ford was cute as a button but not at all my type. I thought to earlier when I told Donette I didn't know my type. It sure wasn't Ford. I'd go out with Grady before I would a pretty boy like Ford. Party with him? Had that even been a question? I didn't know, so I didn't answer. We'd just made it to the entrance to the parking garage anyway. While I tried to remember what level I parked on, I heard a motorcycle roar in the distance. "About those bikers?" I started as my thoughts shifted back to Ford not even

attempting to help me out of that stressful situation earlier. I didn't quite know how to approach the topic, but I was seriously put off.

"The Royal Bastards MC? Got our boss Grady to thank for them hanging around. He's been buddying up to them. Before we know it, he'll be one of them."

"Really? Grady, a biker?"

"We'll be a biker bar before you know it. I'll quit if it comes to that."

I sputtered a laugh. Grady didn't own Bootsies, so I doubted that would ever happen. "You really don't like these guys?" In my experience bikers were generally harmless no matter how tough they put on. And I knew for a fact most people assumed all bikers were bad people.

"I got a sister who runs with them. She keeps a black eye. Nuff said. Seriously though, a girl like you, pretty girl like you." Ford paused and cleared his throat. "Could get abducted out here alone on the streets at night."

"That's why Donette and I walk together." Just as I said it, Ford hit the ground. Someone had hit him in the back of the head. A man in a ski mask emerged from the dark holding a black sack like he was trick-or-treating. Lordalmighty. It dawned on me that I was the treat. He planned to put a hood over my head and abduct me. Just like with old man Henry, I lifted my knee and kicked hard.

Hitting him square in the balls with the pointed toe of my cowboy boot, I watched the man fall forward. Taking off like a deer, I darted through the garage, up the levels to my Gran's vintage orange 84' El Camino, climbed inside and locked the door before I tried to start her up. As usual it took a couple attempts. When she purred to life, like a bat out of hell, I sped through the parking garage to the exit. Luckily, the bar was up, and I didn't have to pay to leave. I was on the highway before I thought of poor Ford. I called Grady. He didn't answer.

As I drove, I texted him real quick. "I need you now." I called again and got an answer. I relayed what had happened and where to find Ford.

Grady said he was on it. "You want to come back and file a police report?"

"No." All I wanted was to take a shower and go to bed.

CHAPTER 2

EVE

"Eve," the old hag hollered from my doorway. Gran banged on the wooden frame. "Eve Angel. Whore. It's well past one."

Waking up in the middle of the afternoon might as well have been illegal around here. What did she expect when I worked until three a.m.? I rose like the dead, took my time with it. Throwing on my robe and slippers, I cleaned myself up before I left my room. Heaven forbid Gran saw me with my hair a mess and crust in my eyes. I heard my Gran groan from her seat when I finally reached the kitchen. I'd gone straight to the counter. People treated you like a low life if you weren't up with the chickens, even if you worked nights in Nashville, Tennessee apparently.

"I wish you could find a normal job. Whore," my Gran complained as I made her lunch, a simple sandwich. I'd left her breakfast in the fridge. I wasn't sure how she managed to heat it up herself if she couldn't put ham and cheese between two slices of bread. See, she could. Frannie

Newberry was a capable woman at seventy, but I had to earn my keep around here and that meant doting on my dad's cruel mouthed mother. Now, that was cruel of me. My Gran was not very nice, a real bitch at times, but bless her heart, she had a real medical condition.

"You know the bars ain't open this early, Fran." Heaven forbid I call her a Gran. She insisted on Fran. Not to mention some honky-tonks were open already and folks were already singing down on Broadway, but what she didn't know wouldn't hurt her. Nights were where I made my money. And I had to make money since I planned to move out of here real soon.

"I meant a normal job. One closer. Whore."

Ignoring the latter, the whore part, I replied, "There ain't nobody wanting to go and listen to anyone a pickin' first thing in the morning." Tourists maybe but not anyone who counts.

"You could work mornings like normal folk, good folk and then go play your music in the afternoon. Whore. They're hiring up at the Walmart. Whore."

I leaned against the counter. "The music scene ain't just playing, it's about listenin'. And being present. About rubbing elbows. For that, I need to be out at night."

"You're your mama up one side and down the other. She was always a dreamin'. Little good it did her. Whore.

And how would you know? You've only been here a couple years. I've lived here my whole life. Whore. And I'm not no damned star yet. Whore."

"You've lived here in Cottontown, Gran... Fran. You ain't stepped foot in the city in a coon's age."

"Cottontown is close enough."

I opened my mouth.

"I'd watch what I say if I were you. Your daddy's askin' after you. Whore. He wants you to come on home. Be done with this foolishness. Go to college like your brother, Hob."

Tapping my foot, I held my tongue.

"You're going to miss me when I'm dead and gone," Gran howled like she always did.

Despite my Gran harping on me, running away to Cottontown had been the best thing to happen to me. After all, I was a skip and a jump from Nashville now. When I didn't argue, Gran sniggered, took her plate, mumbled some more obscenities that she couldn't help, and shuffled back to her room to watch her reality television. To be preached to by a woman who sat in her pajamas and watched "Kardashians" all day when all I wanted to do was sing a song or two at work, maybe be discovered... I screamed internally. But if I shut my mouth, Gran laid off me. That's something that rarely happened back home with dad. A drunk, there was no way he'd let go of an argument until he passed out. He wanted me in college. I'd hated school with a passion. As soon as I turned eighteen, I begged to come live with my Gran. Dad wouldn't have it. After I graduated high school, there was no stopping me from leaving Arkansas to pursue my dream of becoming a Country Music Star.

Dreams... we all woke up from them eventually.

When Gran left the room, Killer clomped in. Our old black Great Dane was no killer, not of live things anyway. He loved to chew up shoes and anything that didn't put up a fight, but Gran kept the name he came with. I let him out to do his business. He was so feeble that he'd be right back in to sleep the day away. Once I poured some coffee that was brewed this morning, popped it into the microwave and grabbed a banana, I glanced at the calendar. Halloween had snuck up on me. Fall always came out of nowhere. Summertime shined so bright that I'd forget there was much else. I was always happiest when I could throw on my bikini and hit the pool. Those times were few and far between now that I was an adult. All of a sudden, before I really got the chance to enjoy the warm weather, boom, the leaves were dead and falling off the trees. Boot and jacket weather was upon us. That made me smile for a moment. Something else that made me smile, all the little children would be coming to the door tonight when Gran liked to turn off her lights. She'd get so pissed off and cuss them all

out. Some of it she would even mean. I hope she didn't pull her gun again. Too bad I'd miss it. I had to work.

Every year at Bootsies, they had a big costume party. I assumed the costume party was annual. I'd only worked at Bootsies for a year and a half. Everybody had to dress up, even the patrons, even my boss Grady. Especially a barmaid like me. Yeah, I was a waitress. Server if you were being polite about it. But every once in a while, I gotta get up on stage, pick my guitar and sing one of my songs. But more often than not, I gotta get up on stage and sing somebody else's song. Grady loved the covers. And the only reason I sang at all was because Grady liked me. And when I say he liked me, he liked, liked me. But he was a fifty-year-old man, and I was 20 years old.

Last year I went as Eve because of my name, Eve Angel Newberry. The punny costume had been my bestie Donette's bright idea. Since I'd not thought of anything else it looked like I'd be going as Eve again. It was better than the other idea Donette had, an angel, since out of everyone who worked at Bootsies, I was the innocent one who didn't smoke, drink or do any drugs. They suspected I wasn't too experienced in bed, as well, and they were right, even though I would never admit it. I grabbed a bright red apple from the fruit bowl. Maybe I'd find an Adam like Donette planned to find her Beetlejuice.

Dreaming again...

I'd not had as much as a date since I arrived in Nashville. No suitors in almost two years. My dry spell started as me trying to take my music seriously for once but turned into a curse. Already, I only had a couple boyfriends to speak of. Back home, it'd been my tragic loss of my mother and overbearing and suspected father that kept guys away from me. Here, I'd done it to myself. Just like I'd gotten stage fright, I had date fright.

Sipping my coffee, I strolled to the screen door. Out of it there were trees as far as the eye could see. Cottontown called itself a rural paradise. It got the rural part right. With approximately four hundred folks living here, it was rural, complete with farmland and curvy back roads. Cottontown reminded me of my home in Arkansas without the drama from my daddy's drinking. Inhaling the fresh air, I knew soon I'd have to don my disguise. Not only would I be dressing up for Halloween, nightly I pretended I didn't mind being groped. Guys got drunk and I looked good. It was bound to happen. Hell, girls got drunk too and fancied me as well. Though that wasn't how my bread was buttered. Needless to say, I'd be putting on my thick skin to head to the bar. Too bad I couldn't put on that skin to sing.

When I moved here, I was told, Nashville drivers were like New York drivers. Yeah, if New York drivers were rednecks with a heap of dead deer in the back of their larger-than-life trucks. Dude just cut me off. Road rage overtaking me, I used my horn way too many times heading to the heart of Nashville, Broadway. And traffic must be

worse here with the unending construction. Entering the city, I spotted fifty-eleven cranes in the skyline at least. Nashville was growing by leaps and bounds. Everyone complained about it, but I'd never known the city any other way. Some called it Cashville, and I liked that name because it was where I made my money. I passed the old Gibson guitar factory before I turned down Church Street and parked in the garage. I hauled my Gibson in its case, the one my mother left me, out of Gran's El Camino and practically ran down the stairs thinking of last night.

I hoped Ford was okay.

Stepping out on the street, right away I heard Broadway, "The Devil Went Down to Georgia" playing to be exact. But it being Halloween, the song had a spooky beat. Then, a big box truck zoomed by and almost hit me. Flipping him off, I thought of how I used to get here early and head the opposite direction, straight for the cupcake vending machine or to get a one-hundred-layer donut. Then I'd head to the Music City Walk of Fame. I'd eat my sweet treat and read the names in the stars on the concrete. That was back when my dreams were fresh. As it was now, I passed the Ryman Auditorium and Legends Corner and didn't even look at the iconic mural with Country Music's biggest stars. Yes, I was ashamed I'd not done more with the opportunity.

Bootsies, a divey place with some of the best musicians one would ever hear was in the historic part of lower Broad. Called Redneck Vegas for a reason with neon signs and the streets packed, Broadway consisted of a very long row of honky-tonks blaring out music from morning to night. All the bars were close together, people streaming in and out and back into another since there were no cover charges. Indeed, we all survived on tips, the musicians, and the ones like me who kept the Tennessee whiskey and beer a flowing. At only three in the afternoon, everyone was already hammered. Even the streets were made for it, Broadway had a barn's dance, we called it. Like the one in Japan, a pedestrian scramble intersection stopped all the traffic and allowed everyone to cross the street in all directions at once. Great for the drunks.

Kid Rock's place had to be the loudest. All kinds of famous folks had bars on Broadway, or at least their name on one. There was a rooftop rat race going. The new bars had multiple levels and rooftop bars with each level featuring a different band, a different genre. Usually on the first floor, there'd be Country music, giving our tourists the Nashville vibe they craved. On the second floor, there'd be some R&B, Rap, you name it. The third floor and the rooftops were wild cards. Older buildings like Bootsies only had one functioning floor but were scrambling to renovate their upstairs and rooftops to compete.

We weren't the only ones going all out for Halloween. Jack-o-lanterns lined the streets and people were already in costume. When I reached Bootsies I heard our third act, the Hillbellas playing Lorrie Morgan's "My Night to Howl". Hillary the lead singer could be seen

through the store front. She'd dressed up like a witch. Like most the bars, the stage was in the window to draw in the customers. Tonight would be filled with Halloweeny songs, anything with spooky references. I peered in but kept walking. Going around the corner, I passed the dumpsters and used the back-alley entrance.

"Beetlejuice, Beetlejuice, Beetlejuice." In her red wedding gown, Donette tried to make her mystery man appear while she rolled silverware in the dish room. I'd brought in a tray of limes to prep. Her Lydia Deetz was perfect.

"How'd you get your bangs like that?" I asked her.

"Hairspray. Lots of it. I've got to look good for my Beetlejuice."

"Didn't you go home with someone last night?" I'd known she had.

"No. He came to mine." Donette lived nearby in a condo downtown.

"And?" I pressed because she didn't go on.

"If you moved in with me, you'd know all about it already."

I'd planned to move in, was on the lease and paid half the rent already. I had a new bed and some of my belongings moved in too, but I didn't know how to break it to Gran. "Soon. After Thanksgiving, I promise."

Donette groaned.

"You know my Gran needs me. So, what about him? Didn't it work out?"

"He's fine." She waved off my question.

"Then why are you looking for another guy?"

"Let's just say the guy I was with last night is kind of unavailable."

"He's with someone?"

"No. We're just fuckbuddies."

My face scrunched up.

"He's not looking for a relationship," Donette said as a matter of fact. "Well, actually, he's in a few. Total Alpha male, I tell you. He still sees his ex and a few girls. I'm one of them."

"How does that work?"

Donette rolled her eyes at me.

"What about love, Donette?"

"Girl, I love hard and fuck harder. You know that." That was Donette's catchphrase. "Eve, you need to get laid. At least once."

"I know. But the right guy," I started.

"If I waited for the right guy... At least get some practice in, girl."

As bad as it sounded, Donette was right. I was hard up. I'd not been with a guy in almost two years, and we hadn't done much of anything except heavy petting.

"Eve, you've got to stop letting fear rule your life. I know you have some issues from childhood, your dad killing your mom and all, but you're way too sexy to be going home and dialing a rotary phone every night."

It took me a minute to realize she meant masturbating. "I don't go home and do that. And my dad, he didn't. Just everyone thinks so." I didn't want to talk about my dad or about my mom's murder.

"Whatever. You could snap your fingers and have anyone in here. You know that, right? Just like you could be singing anywhere in this town if you weren't so fucking scared."

I ignored the part about singing. We'd been over it too many times. "It ain't smart to leave with just anybody."

"You've got a key to our apartment. Pick some guy and bring him over. You could be waiting a lifetime for the right dick to come along."

"You're right. I'm still waiting for the right dick to come along."

Donette got loud, "Bless your heart. I don't see how you do it. I can't go a week without a dick in my mouth."

I slapped her with my bar towel, but she was right.

Grady came over after he heard Donette. He joined us to roll. "What are we talking about?"

The knife slipped, and I sliced my hand. "Ouch." I held up my bloody hand to show them.

Donette ignored my injury. Her voice was dry. "Getting Eve laid."

Grady made a face. Standing, he took my hand and me over to the sink to run it under water. He rubbed the bloody cut and looked me in the eyes, "You need to get laid, Eve. Life's too short to wait for the right guy." Then he cleared his throat and changed the subject. "Did you hear about my surprise?"

"I did. What is it?"

Grady pulled gauze and tape from his apron and wrapped my hand up. "That's not how surprises work."

He'd dressed as the wolfman which was great with his grey hair and beard. Celie was a sight as the bride of Frankenstein. She'd even done the big, tall hair. Once we finished with the silverware, the two of them got on stage between the third and fourth act for a duet, John Prine's, "In Spite of Ourselves." Their rendition was a classic at Bootsies, but also a bitter reminder that they used to be in love.

Behind the bar, Nikki, our day bartender waited to be relieved. She'd been slinging drinks all day as a scary clown. Ford showed up late. Who could blame him after getting knocked out last night? He'd dressed as a member of the Tennessee Titans, big surprise. In the same jersey he wore yesterday, he'd thrown on white sweatpants instead of his normal jeans, pushed them up to his knees and painted a black stripe under his eyes.

"Are you okay?" I asked him.

Reaching up, he scrubbed the back of his head.

"Who would do such a thing?" I declared.

"Probably one of those bikers."

Jasper came in even later, saying he was a lumberjack. He'd simply worn a flannel with his normal jeans and t-shirt. Bless him. His cornbread's not done in the middle. He limped over.

"What's wrong with you?" I asked him.

"Someone ran over my foot."

"Lordalmighty. You serious?" There wasn't a day that went by that I didn't almost get hit by a car walking to work.

Viv and Greta were dressed as Playboy bunnies, one red and one purple, but they put the bunny ears up through a cowboy hat. Both had on those body suits with a thong. At least they wore nude tights. They'd rake in the tips tonight. Not that they didn't every other night. I didn't want to be mean, but Greta was so trashy she better not linger by the curb on garbage day. Viv had gotten so much work done she could donate her body to Tupperware when she died. I had no idea how she could afford it. Well, that was a lie. Viv had expensive tastes in men.

The barmaids were all a sexy version of something, a sexy nurse, a sexy maid, a sexy female firefighter, a sexy Freddy Krueger, a sexy cowgirl. I simply wore my white dress from homecoming Senior year and kept a red apple in my pocket to pull out when people asked who I was. Last year, I had a bunch of fake ivy and a stuffed animal snake to wrap around my arm too, but our dog Killer done ate them.

Our kitchen staff came as Joe Exotic zombies, every last one of them. Wearing blond mullets, pink button up shirts and cowboy hats, they had done their faces as the living dead. Well, all of them except Jennifer our one female cook who came as an undead Carol Baskin. She put the fake blonde, braided wig up in a hairnet and looked hilarious.

The patrons had to be in costume to enter. Not really. We couldn't make them, but we had a creepy, red lettered sign that said as much. Some of them had gone all out like the scary twins from the Shining but some claimed to be Randy Travis or George Jones because they wore a cowboy hat and boots. There were a few Rebas and Dollys too.

While I ran drinks, something caught my eye. Lordalmighty. From the back wall, a man watched me. I always noticed that sort of thing. A girl had to keep an eye out for men creeping on her and all. However, with this one, I stopped dead in my tracks and stared back. My breath hit the road, and my knees gave out at the sight of him. This bearded man donned a pair of black angel wings as big as life. Shirtless, he showed off his gorgeous bod with a tattoo across his bicep and chest. That was it. That was his costume. Otherwise, he wore distressed, faded jeans with a proper belt buckle and black cowboy boots. It was the best damned costume I'd seen all night. He was so hot he made my teeth sweat. This man was the gosh darn best looking man I'd ever seen in my life, hands down and nipples up. Yes, my nipples got hard just seeing him.

Ding Dong, he won. Only he stared at me like I was the prize. I gulped and felt a trickle of wetness in my undergarments. I tried to play off our staring contest like it was nothing. On my way to deliver two drafts, I knew I'd have to walk past him. I worried for the first time tonight about my hair. I hadn't been able to do a thing with it before work and by now it probably looked like a cat had been sucking on it. Sweating like a stripper on Sunday, I'd been busier than a chicken running from Colonel Sanders. When I almost made it past him, the angel stepped in front of me. Rocking to a stop, I nearly spilled the beers.

"Lord have mercy," I complained.

He took the beers from my stunned hands. Face to face with his hard nipples, I lifted my chin to see his face. The dark angel smiled down at me with a grin so wickedly sexy that my mouth watered even more. Not only that, his glorious brown eyes smiled too as they searched mine, mesmerizing me for a moment.

"Have a drink with me." His rough voice grabbed a hold of me as he handed me back a beer.

I shook my head trying to shake the spell. "I can't. I work here." I took both beers back. "These are for somebody else."

The fallen angel stole the mugs back. "Sure, you can. Who's going to notice?" His voice bellowed, sending chills through me.

We were awful close, so close I could feel the heat rising off his bare torso. He stepped back a ways, and I noticed the dark hair traveling down his tight abs. The curls looked like they went all the way down. I imagined the rest wondering if the right dick had finally come along.

He spoke again, drawing my eyes back up to his face. "Pardon me. I've not introduced myself. I'm Hallow and you're dressed as Eve, right? It's All Hallows' Eve. Halloween. It's meant to be. You and me."

Good manners were never out of style, and I found I liked him even more. "How did you know I'm Eve?" I hadn't shown him my apple.

"I asked around. We're going to have a drink." He wasn't asking. Pushing the other beer in my hand, he winked and cracked his glass against mine. "Holler and swaller."

"I don't believe in fate," I said as I gave in and crashed my glass against his. I threw back the beer like I knew what I was doing. Boy, how I needed a drink of something, but I didn't drink. Only twenty years old and having my license to serve open alcohol, I tried my best to follow Grady's rules at the bar even though the other girls my age didn't. From the smell of it, I never thought I'd like the taste of beer, but the ice-cold Oktoberfest hit the spot. I almost chugged the whole damned thing.

"I don't believe in fate either. Well, I didn't until I saw you."

What a line? I about choked on my beer.

The dark angel watched me, smirking. "What happened to your hand?"

Glancing at it, I noticed the blood seeping through the bandage. I'd have to change it soon. "Oh, this. Knife accident." I told myself to ask him something back. *Come on, Eve. Don't blow this!* "You're some sort of what? Fallen Angel?"

"Yes, that's the costume. But the name's Hallow."

"You've got to be shitting me."

"Nah. Everyone calls me Hallow."

"Hallow," I said the word again and thought about its meaning. It meant holy, saintly, virtuous. My eyes squinted. "You religious or something?"

"No. Far from it." He chuckled like that was a ridiculous notion. "Are you?"

"Maybe a little." My head fell sideways, and my hand went to my hip. "How'd you get that name then?"

"Let's just say I've fallen far from grace. How low can you go, some asked me. It turned into Hallow. What can I say, my friends are assholes."

"Sounds like it."

"What's your name?"

We didn't wear name tags, and I usually didn't tell patrons my name. But Hallow was something else. My

guard slipped down. The simper on my face burned my cheeks. "I'm Eve."

"I mean, your real name?"

On second thought, I decided not to tell him that Eve was my real name. I mustered some defenses. "What's your real name?" Hallow was clearly a nickname.

"Eve's a nice name."

I noticed he'd changed the subject fast. A guy dressed in a full-on bedazzled Elvis costume joined Hallow, the dark angel, and I changed my mind about Hallow winning a costume contest. Elvis was alive and, in the building, albeit in his aged and overweight state. Hallow put his arm around this Elvis. "This here's my buddy, Dimple. Dimple, this is Eve."

Dimple, no, Elvis seized my hand and bent to kiss it. His lips curled against my skin. His pompadour and sideburns were impeccable. My knees wobbled for a different reason this time because the man genuinely resembled the King. I said as much, and he replied, "Thank you. Thank you very much." He winked at me on his way up.

Past him, I spotted Grady watching me from the bar. I finished my beer in one gulp and made my excuses. "I've got to get back to work." I'd have to go ask for more beers, too.

Hallow stopped me, his warm hand soft on my bicep. "When do you get off work?"

"I'm not sure. When business dies down." That was the truth. I wasn't closing so until Celie or Grady cut the floor, I wouldn't know.

"I'll be waiting. I'm not leaving without you," Hallow said as a matter of fact.

I laughed as I walked away. I didn't know if I was scared or seriously turned on.

CHAPTER 3

HALLOW

Eve... I searched her big brown eyes, but she didn't recognize me. Coming to Bootsies in costume had been the best idea. Only Dimple agreed to come with me though. One of the best Elvis impersonators in these parts, he lived in costume. Hell, my brother lived as Elvis, but thankfully I talked him into leaving his cut at home tonight, something unheard of for a member of the Royal Bastards MC. My President only gave his permission because it was his favorite holiday. But Eve had said she didn't date nasty bikers.

"Why do you give a fuck?" My buddy Thorn asked me when I'd asked him to come to the honky-tonk.

"I don't give a fuck. Not really. But won't it be fun to make this chic fall in love with me and then tell her I'm a Royal Bastard?"

Thorn replied, "I'm sure she'll agree you're a bastard. Won't she recognize you?"

"Nah, man, look." I'd cut and trimmed my beard close to my face.

"Look the same to me. All y'all look the same."

I didn't tell Thorn that last night I went to bed dreaming of this woman. There'd been something about her, more than the fact she'd not given me a second glance. When she bumped into me, and I caught her, my dick stood at attention at the sight of her, yeah. Pretty petite blonde with her shirt tied up, showing off her tiny, tan navel with her long legs on display. I was sure I wasn't the only guy to notice. However, my heart skipped a beat when I stared into her deep soulful eyes. That had never happened to me before. Fuck, I thought about getting my chest looked at. I could've killed my ex-girlfriend Steph for threatening her, a mere stranger. An animal in me wanted to protect this strange girl, wanted to have her as my own. I never believed in love at first sight until I saw her. Still didn't know if I believed.

When she wiped the whiskey from my cheek, I thought I had a chance. But she didn't take to me and said she didn't date nasty bikers, shattering my brief hopes. I hung around after my brothers left. And when Eve stepped on stage and sang like an angel in heaven, I truly fell in love. Her voice reached in and ripped my heart out. Starstruck, I wanted to talk to her afterwards, but Wolf asked me to get lost. When I chose these black angel wings, I thought of her. Eve the angel. I was no angel, not anymore. The black wings

bared my evil soul, but I would fly to heaven to be at her side. These were things I wouldn't dare tell my brothers.

"Sounds asinine, a waste of time, when you could be here at Royal Road at the real party," Thorn added.

He was right. Broadway had its honky-tonks and bright lights. They called it Nashvegas and the only things missing were the strip clubs and casinos. One might find all those things in the city elsewhere, but for all that and then some, for the real Nashvegas, folks had to head to Royal Road, the playground of the Royal Bastards MC's Nashville Chapter. And they had to be invited. We weren't no two-bit tourist trap. Royal Road was an exclusive experience reserved for the well connected, meaning connected to the club and our President Kingpin. That included everyone from low lives to celebrities.

When I patched over to the Nashville Chapter from Charleston, I'd gone in blind, not knowing what the hell I'd be getting into. I'd been used to a club that resembled a tight knit family with wives and kids always around. Fuck, it'd been getting to be a bit much at times. Couldn't walk to the bar without watching your step. Someone's crotch goblin might have been underfoot. You thought bikers were mean, wait till their ol' lady said you looked at her funny. The fuckers in Charleston had started breeding like rabbits. When I'd become one of them, they were all about partying. But that wasn't why I left. Hell, I'd loved to have found me an ol' lady and had a few babies running around their roadhouse. After all, I'd made some great friends in Viking, Prodigy, and Smoke.

My best buddy Smoke warned me that Royal Road was nothing like the Devil's Playground. "You couldn't pay me to patch over to Kingpin." He'd just gotten divorced, so I thought he just wanted me to stay and party with him. "But you were a city slicker. Maybe you'll fit in."

Yeah, I was from Cleveland, Ohio originally and ran to the hills of West Virginia to hide. My troubles found me there. Once that fucker Justice Masters started sniffing around, I had to get away. If Detective Masters found out who I was, he would try to blackmail me and that could've put the club in jeopardy. Murder, my old President, agreed it'd be best if I left Charleston and tried a bigger chapter. Even in Nashville, I was too close to home, but this city was bigger, and the club was bigger too. I wouldn't be making a name for myself. I planned to stay hidden.

Smoke had been right. The Royal Bastards MC in Nashville was an enterprise, more business than family, not that my brothers weren't still loyal to each other, loyal to a fault, but money mattered a whole lot more. More money, more problems, they say. And no one wanted their kids coming to Royal Road. Most kept their ol' ladies away, too. There was another clubhouse solely for them, a lot more lowkey. No serious girlfriend to speak of, needless to say, I'd never been.

Kingpin ran a tight ship. He'd spent six years of his life in prison for a crime he didn't commit and another year for one he did. Thought he was Johnny Cash or something now, though. Always had some story about being in the big house. Accused of being a drug lord in his twenties, he'd simply been an informant for the police. The detectives turned around and pinned the whole thing on him, hence the name. Man earned major notoriety for being a kid accused of running such a lucrative illicit organization. He became so famous, eventually, the real crime boss got jealous and confessed. Kingpin, finally proved innocent, was let loose with a big settlement, but as soon as he got to Nashville, he shot his twin brother in the hind end. When our President was released a second time, he joined the Royal Bastards MC here in Music City and quickly built an empire that catered to people who could pay for the privilege to party. To really party. The dirty deeds done at Royal Road actually stayed there. You couldn't kill a man in Vegas and the law not follow you home. With my background, I had to turn a blind eye to most of it. Part of me no longer cared if rules were broken, but when people were hurt, my old instincts kicked in. Good thing I had my brothers to kick my ass when that happened. Put me in my place. Thankfully, nothing happened here that I couldn't stomach. I knew a thing or two about real atrocities. Kingpin was an outlaw not a monster.

Now, I was an outlaw too. And I'd not let myself get too close to a woman, not in Charleston and not here. Not emotionally anyway. Since joining the Royal Bastards MC, I had more pussy than I could shake a stick at. But when it came to matters of the heart, I'd left it in Ohio when I left my life there. Steph, that bitch had been a mistake. A fuck buddy who'd gotten confused and thought she owned me. I let our non-relationship go on too long. She sure didn't have my heart, and the pussy hadn't been great either. I'd just been tired of having a new woman every week.

Getting Eve to have a drink with me, I put that mess behind me. I knew I didn't want this angel to fly away. I'd been watching her all evening, waiting for her to come to me, I didn't think I'd get tired of her too soon. Blonde and tiny with curves in all the right places, I could only imagine how great she'd look naked riding me like that Mechanical Bull over in the corner. I'd asked around and another waitress told me she was dressed as Eve. Fuck, what luck since my road name was Hallow, and it was fucking Halloween, aka All Hallows' Eve. When Eve zoomed my way delivering two frosty mugs of beer, I saw my chance. I stepped in front of her, took the beers and insisted she have a drink with me.

"Lord have mercy," she exclaimed. I'd stopped her mid-marathon. Her chest heaved, making her amble breasts quake in the thin white dress that she wore the hell out of. Did she know I could see her pink peaks through the sheer fabric? Her shy nervous grin answered, probably not. Her face reddened as I watched her pant. Eve's skin glistened with sweat. This was exactly how I wanted her to look, writhing under me as I pierced her with my cock later.

Her pretty brown eyes were eating me up as she took me in. I stepped back a bit so she could see all of me including the huge woody in my jeans. Girl was impressed with me shirtless, and I felt I had this in the bag.

"Pardon me. I've not introduced myself. I'm Hallow and you're dressed as Eve, right? It's All Hallows' Eve. Halloween. It's meant to be. You and me." The line was cheesy as hell. Eve laughed, and I'd not heard anything better in a long time. Like her singing voice, her laugh was angelic. When she replied that she didn't believe in fate, I liked her all the more. I didn't believe in any of that shit either. No matter how my chest fluttered when I saw Eve last night, I knew for certain now, I wanted her in my bed.

She sucked down a beer like a pro, and I pictured her sucking something else. Then I noticed her hand. I'd watched her bust her ass all night and had no idea she been injured. Eve played it off like it was nothing, but a storm rumbled in me. Just like the night before, I wanted to protect her, not just from my crazy ex but from working her ass off in this dive, with a hurt hand no less. Fuck, I'd be having a talk with Wolf as soon as I saw him.

Dimple showed up and stole the show as usual. The fat fuck kept a lady on his lap.

"Don't get any ideas," I said to him when Eve walked away.

He tugged on his pant's waist, telling me, "I've already gotten blown by the Shining Twins over there."

Two creepy as hell twins in blue dresses waved at him from afar. Raising my eyebrows, I patted his back. "You're the King."

"Damn straight. Everyone wants to suck Elvis's fat dong. Still don't get why we're here. Kingpin goes all out for Halloween."

"You owe me." I'd done him a good turn just last week, covering for him on a run when he was too high to ride. If he didn't watch it, he'd end up like the real Elvis.

Dimple kept going on about all we were missing at Royal Road, the naked bobbing for apples, the Halloween candy buffet laid on strippers, the masquerade orgy.

None of that mattered to me. The waitress dressed as Eve conquered my thoughts.

CHAPTER 4

EVE

Hallow and I stole glances at each other all evening, but I hadn't been back his way. My nerves had gotten the better of me. Knowing I was being watched, my stomach filled with butterflies. The Halloween tunes continued as the band sang, "Elvira", "Bad Moon Rising", "Little Red Riding Hood", and "Feed my Frankenstein" in between everyone's favorite country hits, like Chris Stapleton's "Tennessee Whiskey". Jackie's Heroes snuck in their original songs too. Before I knew it the crowd had worn thin.

Donette and I huddled. "The gorgeous demon, huh?"

"Not a demon. A fallen angel."

"Same thing," she countered. "An alpha male for sure. Watch out."

"He wants to know when I get off. Actually, he said he's not leaving without me."

"Jaylynn said you're closing for her. Fuck me, that's hot. He's going to fuck your brains out. I bet."

"Dern. I told her I would." I'd forgotten all about telling Jaylynn I'd close. I didn't comment on the fucking my brains out part as I watched two zombies dance.

"You'll have to let that demon know you'll be late. Or you could ask Grady if you can go early."

My nerves threatening to hold me back, I walked over to let the fallen angel know I wouldn't be available tonight. A drunk vampire stopped me.

"I'm on break. Someone else will get your order," I said as loud as I could.

He found my ear and said, "Hey, baby. Want to suck on something."

"No. Get lost." I shooed him away, but he didn't budge.

"Just a nibble."

The jerk opened his mouth to reveal blunt plastic fangs. He snatched my arms and leaned into my neck. Shit, this drunk was really going to bite me. I punched at his back just as a dark angel loomed over us. Hallow yanked the guy off me and hauled back and hit him in the chin. The vampire fell to the ground like a sack of potatoes.

"Holy cow. You didn't have to knock him out," I shouted. "But thanks. I was coming over here to tell you I'm not getting off anytime soon. I'm closing, sorry."

"I can wait," Hallow replied. The vampire wasn't out, he grumbled some obscenities from the floor. Hallow kicked his side, a bit too hard. He was going to break the creep's rips.

"You can't wait if you're kicked out of here for fighting." I looked around for our bouncer, knowing he'd boot both Hallow and the vampire out.

Hallow reached down and helped the vampire to his feet. "Next time don't mess with my girl."

Ignoring the my girl part, I spun on my heels heading back to the bar.

I searched for Donette so I could tell her what had happened, but she'd disappeared. In all my time at Bootsies, only our bouncers had stopped a patron from accosting me. A smile took over my face while I replayed the scene in my head. Once I spotted my bestie, there was some sort of ruckus near the front door. Wondering if Hallow and the vampire were fighting again, I stood on my tiptoes to get a glimpse. It wasn't Hallow. It was the bikers from last night. They were back. The music lulled. The biggest one shot his gun at the floor, and it stopped all together. Between the gunshot and the screams, the whole place, everyone screeched to a halt. We all froze.

The biker with the gun turned to the band. "Youin's pack on up and get."

Our fourth act, Jackie's Heroes were out of the door in one minute flat while everyone else waited on pins and needles. They left their tips behind. Where was Grady? Where was our bouncer, big Earl? He didn't usually go home until Grady cut the floor. Had Grady sent anyone home? I tapped my foot waiting for someone to do something. I started to step forward as the biker announced, "No one else is getting out of here until we find out who killed our buddy... Grady."

Grady? Dead? No, I didn't believe it. I'd just seen him, though it was hours ago. We'd been busy so if I hadn't seen him, he could've been in the kitchen helping out. But as long as whiskey flowed Grady would be here.

As a biker blocked the front door, the head one went on, loud enough for us all to hear, "We'll be having a look around so prepare yourself to be questioned. No funny business. No phone calls. You hear? If you cooperate, this will be over in no time, and no one will get hurt."

The three dozen or so bar patrons were all a stir, but I noticed all the employees were here. All of us. Grady hadn't sent anyone home. Now we were all locked in while some bikers tried to find a killer. Ford motioned me to the bar. I joined him behind it wanting to ask him if this was what Grady had instore for us, a murder mystery party?

"Grady murdered. I wonder who did it?" Ford said right off the bat, but not like he was upset or too surprised.

"Who, indeed? Maybe it was you," I said, playing along.

Ford grimaced. "That's not funny."

The biker's voice called out again asking if anyone could occupy the stage for a while. I guess the nervous silence had gotten to them. Before I could grab my guitar, that Elvis character was on stage, calling up anyone who could play. Ford shook his finger at me, warning me to stay put. Greta and Viv agreed that we shouldn't call attention to ourselves.

Viv said, "They pulled a gun. I'm sure someone's called the cops already. We've all got cell phones."

Ford asked, "Are you going to?"

"Not on my life," Viv said. "And my phone's in my locker like it's supposed to be. Besides, I don't want no trouble. I'm on probation."

Greta chimed in, "Jackie's Heroes will dial 911, no doubt. This is a hostage situation."

"I wonder why they let the band leave?" I asked.

Ford answered me, "They don't want to upset anyone who matters, and a band around here could have connections to someone important. Bass player John's cousin, James Earl writes music for that band who opened for Keith Urban last month."

Maybe, but it all seemed a little too organized to me.

Greta said, "Any of us could have connections."

Viv rebutted, "You're kidding, right? We work here, remember. It's one in the morning. The customers left are probably all tourists. If not, they are someone preying on tourists or they're drunks."

That was a bit harsh but likely true.

Greta said, "Bar next door might call the cops too. I'm sure they heard the gunshot."

Ford's eyes rolled back. "Like a gunshot is unusual 'round here."

"Grady didn't send anyone home," I mentioned. "Anyone seen him?"

We all chimed in that we just saw him at least within the last hour or so. All the other employees seemed to stay put wherever they'd been. I wondered if the bikers had warned people to stay put, and I'd missed it. However, Ford had the barmaids trained well to stay off the bar. Though, he never minded me being here. I thought about him asking to party with me last night briefly before it dawned on me why Ford didn't scare me away from the bar. Like Grady,

Ford was sweet on me. He'd even changed clothes and wiped off the football makeup thinking we might party tonight. It was a good thing not too many men worked here. I wondered if Jasper had a thing for me too. Not the handsomest, he was a bit slow, at least I thought, because he didn't talk much. He mixed a fine drink though and fast. Not only that, he was the best at the theatrics at the bar. My mind shot to our bouncer, Earl.

"Anyone seen Earl?"

No one had. I couldn't remember if I'd seen him all night. Earl sort of blended into the wall until you needed him. He hadn't come to my rescue moments ago with the vampire.

My eyes searched for the few people I cared for. I saw Celie through the small window to the kitchen. She was talking to someone dressed as Joe Exotic Zombie like they all were. Donette huddled in the corner with her Beetlejuice. I was excited that she'd finally found him. Then, there was someone else on my mind.

On the stage, Elvis… What did Hallow say his name was? Another nickname, Dimple, went into an upbeat, "Devil in Disguise". As he sang just like Elvis, speaking of the devil, I watched Hallow with his big black wings move through the thin crowd. He was coming to me.

"You okay?" Hallow asked when he sat at the bar, his wings taking up three spaces. Now I knew why he'd been against the wall all night.

"Sure, she is," Ford answered him from my side.

"Get lost," I said to Ford, elbowing him in the side. He held up his hands and slinked away to the other side to talk more with his crew. I turned to Hallow and asked, "What do you think about all this?"

He leaned in so I could hear him. "They think the killer is still here. I don't know about that."

"Who? Those bikers? How would you know where the killer is?"

"I know a thing or two."

"Maybe it was you. I've not seen you here before, and I'm taking it, you're not a tourist."

"No, I'm local now. I didn't kill anyone. And by knowing a thing or two. I have some experience with murders. I used to be a cop."

"Used to?"

"Yeah, detective. Not anymore."

A detective? I wondered how old he was. He didn't look a day over twenty-five, maybe twenty-six.

"Grady, he was your boss, right?"

"Yeah. And he was just here. I'd just seen him, though I can't place when or where. It's been so busy in here tonight and everyone is dressed up. It's all so distracting." I'd actually been distracted by him, the sight of him and thinking about meeting him after work. I supposed my work was over now. I certainly wasn't serving any drinks while we were all being held hostage, regardless of whether I believed it or not.

"You know of anyone who wanted him gone?"

"No. Is this an interrogation?"

"The sooner they find the killer, the sooner we can leave."

"We?"

"You were meeting me after you got off, right?"

"I never said that."

"You never said no."

That was true. Clearly, I could have my cake and eat it too. I could see Hallow after work as in right now without having to leave the comfort of Bootsies. After all, there was some sort of party going on. Grady couldn't have been murdered. Why would anyone kill him? The man worked six days a week. Ford said Celie said Grady had a surprise for us all. Grady had mentioned it himself to me, too, when he bandaged my hand. Additionally, he was friends with these bikers, the Royal Bastards MC, according to Ford. All the more reason for them to be in on the surprise. And they let the band leave. Bands have contracts. If they hadn't let them leave Grady would've had to pay them for another set.

Celie came to the bar and declared she'd be serving up Hot Chicken and any draft beer on the house to make up for the inconvenience to our guests, and that we employees could partake as well. "But make sure to ring it in. I'll comp it." Worried about the business, she didn't seem one bit shaken by the death of her ex-husband.

Plus, it was Halloween. What a very Halloweeny thing to do, a surprise Murder Mystery Dinner.

"Want some Hot Chicken?" I asked Hallow.

"Nah, can't stand the stuff."

"Suit yourself." I ordered some. He did want another beer. I ordered myself one too and poured them even though Ford gave me a nasty look. If Grady was dead there was no reason not to drink or make Ford upset. I slid a beer to Hallow. We crashed our drinks together again. The Elvis impersonator sang "Monster Mash", and I was finally settled that we were indeed partying.

"Holler and swaller," Hallow said.

I studied his accent. It was southern but just enough. "You're not from around here, are you?"

"You've got me. The Hot Chicken always gives me away. I'm from Cleveland, Ohio, originally."

"So, a Yankee?"

"Whoa. Not exactly. A buckeye then I moved to West Virginia for a spell. You're not from here. You're from Arkansas."

I put my hands on my hips. "You've been asking around?"

"No. I'm good with accents and tells."

"Cause you're the po-po. How do I know you ain't a cop still? An Undercover Agent?"

"Trust me, I'm far from it."

"Okay. I don't have anything to hide anyhow. I'm from Flipping, Arkansas."

"I didn't mean to offend you."

"No. I'm not cussing. The town is Flipping. It's Flipping, Arkansas."

"Never heard of it."

"Only about a thousand people there."

"What brings you to Nashville?"

Lifting my shoulders, I lied, "Always wanted to sling beer and push peanuts." I sat a bowl of peanuts in front of him.

"You're a singer."

"Is there a tell for that?"

"I asked around. Folks say you have a beautiful voice. You going to kick my buddy Dimple off the stage so I can hear it?"

Blushing, I changed the subject. "So, who do you think killed my boss?"

Before he could answer, Viv dropped off my basket of Hot Chicken and fries. She winked at Hallow, and I watched his gorgeous eyes bob on the bunny tail in the middle of her ass as she walked away.

He noticed me watching him ogle her.

I stuffed my mouth full of fries and said, "You like that? You can have it. She's single." I took another drink of beer, loving how it dissolved my insecurities. I didn't tell him that she wouldn't have him. Viv was a gold digger.

"No, I don't want her." Hallow's hand carefully took my bandaged one, but his eyes bolted to mine as he gave me a serious look. His forehead all crinkled, he smiled at me

again. Damn, his smile was fire. With my mouthful, I returned the grin. His flirtatious eyes searched mine. I'm sure they found a twinkle, but I didn't know what he was looking for. He finally spoke. "I don't know who killed your boss. I need more information."

I took my hand from him to eat my chicken.

"You're eating that stuff with your fingers?"

"Yeah," I said, for the first time wondering if it was unlady-like or something. Or unsanitary since my hand was bandaged. "What's wrong with that?" I licked the hot grease off my fingertips and wiped my hands on my apron.

"It's just so hot. The sauce, I mean. It'll burn your innards. And you're hot too. Way hotter than that chicken. But that stuff ain't fit to eat."

Laughing at that, I picked up the chicken with my hands again. "You know about Hot Chicken?"

"No. I know about fried chicken, chicken and dumplings, Buffalo chicken, Barberton Chicken, we prefer that in northern Ohio."

"Well, Hot Chicken was invented by Prince. Not that Prince with the frilly shirt. A different Prince. I'm sure he had a first name, but I can't think of it. Well, really it was his wife. See, he was cheating on her. She found out and decided to make his dinner, his chicken, extra, extra hot. He liked it so well, he decided to sell it. Don't worry it took

65

about a year of Bootsies serving nothing but Hot Chicken for me to tolerate the stuff. And I'm just starving."

"Eat up." Hallow watched me eat like he'd be popping me in the oven afterwards. "I've been watching you all night. You've not stopped."

"Yeah, I'm exhausted."

"And to think I wanted you to go out tonight. I planned to fuck your brains out."

"Yeah, guys always want to go out after work when I just want to go straight to bed." I'd been speaking on third hand knowledge and before I realized what he just said. "Excuse me?" Had he been talking to Donette? The phrase was commonplace but through me for a loop, anyway.

"Maybe they just want to go to bed with you."

I rolled my eyes. "That's all you're after, a one-night stand."

"No," he answered in such a way I wasn't sure, but he played it off well. "I'll fuck your brains out all the time."

Normally if a man said that to me, I'd run the other way, but coming from Hallow, my body wanted to jump the bar and tackle him. I let my head speak. "I'm not looking for a fuckfriend, sorry."

"A fuckbuddy?"

"Whatever. I'm not looking for one."

"No. I've had that... You've not even agreed to go out with me, remember."

"Well, we're here right now. We can't go anywhere so we might as well find out who the killer is." I put my empty basket into one of the bus tubs and opened a wet nap to clean my hands and mouth. I knew I'd be taking off some of the little makeup I had on in a ring around my lips and found I didn't care. Looking at the bottom of the beer, I'd figured out why people drink.

Hallow lifted my chin. "You're a lightweight. You ought to slow down. We have a killer to find."

"You don't think the killer is here."

"If you killed someone, would you stay?"

"Only if I had to or if I wanted people to think I was innocent."

"I'm sure there's another entrance."

"Yeah, the back. Come on."

CHAPTER 5

EVE

I went around the bar and grabbed Hallow's hand to lead him to our super-secret alley entrance. It was only a secret from inside the bar. Between the restrooms sat what looked like a broom closet, a locked narrow door, but it was never locked. All us employees knew the right way to open it. You had to lift on the handle and turn to the right. The door would pop open eventually. Behind it laid a long hallway leading to the alley. Hallow folded in his wings to fit close to his back as I fiddled with the door. Once it cracked open, I motioned for us to get in quick so we could shut it behind us.

We stepped into darkness. Right away we heard a fuss. I flipped on the light ready to fight. Against the wall, Donette as Lydia Deetz leaned, her bare leg up and around Beetlejuice's backside. His black and white striped pants pooled at his ankles. Her red panties hung from his mouth as he pounded her. She repeated his name over and over while he snarled, his mouth full of red lace. I noticed her exposed breast and turned into Hallow to hide my eyes. He

69

snaked his arm around my back. I'd seen Donette practically naked before, but it'd just dawned on me that I'd walked in on an intimate act.

Unfazed by us, they went on seemingly even harder and faster. My breath hitched as I listened to Donette cry out in ecstasy. Leaning into Hallow's warm chest, my insides yearned to cry out too, though they never had. I could only imagine how she felt. They were still at it. Hallow watched them while I waited, my face pressed against his skin. A good minute passed as Hallow fondled my hair. He might as well have been stroking my pussy with the way it responded.

Glancing up, I whispered, "Maybe we should just leave."

Hallow brushed my hair back and his eyes held a hungry gaze. We were so close I could feel the big D in his pants against me. He liked what he'd seen. After he took a breath, he simpered. "We can leave out the back. Let's get out of here."

"I'm still on the clock."

"Your boss is dead. You said you'd see me after work. Let's blow this joint."

"I can't." I mean, Grady said I needed to get laid. And he couldn't really be dead. But this party had to be his

surprise for us. I couldn't just leave, could I? "I've got to find out who killed Grady."

Hallow seemed content with that. "Yeah, we're supposed to be finding a killer."

"I doubt it's either one of them." Lydia and Beetlejuice were still fucking against the wall. Dern.

"You know'em?"

"That's my best friend, Donette. And Beetlejuice."

"You don't know him?"

"Nope, she just met him."

"Doesn't look like it." Hallow narrowed his eyes.

"That's Donette for you. Bless her heart. I would never."

"Never what? Let a guy you just met fuck you against the wall?"

Stepping back, I crossed my arms. "No."

"Not even me?" He winked and squeezed me back to him.

I put my hands up on his bare chest in protest. We'd gotten too close, too quick. Every ounce of my body begged for him to fuck me against the wall, but my head argued. My heart broke the tie. It didn't want to get broken.

Hallow's arms fell away, but I didn't move from his chest.

Peering down, he lifted my chin. "Are you sure you don't want to leave with me? We don't have to go out. I'll make sure you get home. It's only a matter of time before Riff thinks about the backdoor, and we won't have a way out."

"Riff? You on a first name basis with these bikers?"

Hallow looked away from me to study the scene again. "There were name tags."

"They questioned you?"

"First thing."

"What did you say?"

"I'm just here to party." His eyes returned to my face. "Actually, the truth is, I just hung around waiting on you."

"You didn't tell them that?"

"No. I didn't."

"Did you find out anything?"

"They say Grady's dead body was found in the walk-in freezer about an hour ago."

"Really?" I put my finger to my lips.

"They're thinking it happened after midnight."

"That's a lot of new information."

"You've just got to know what to ask."

"Well, let's go ask around."

"Hold on. Those bikers are already doing that. The killer is not just going to give themselves away," Hallow strained.

"Then what do we do?"

"We'll just go hang out with your coworkers. Who do you think we should start with?"

"I don't think anyone who works here would kill Grady."

"When someone's murdered, the authorities always suspect the wife or the girlfriend."

"His ex-wife works here."

"Anyone else he's dating?"

"No." I didn't want to mention Grady's thing for me. "We'll go talk to Celie."

Donette was still getting it on with Beetlejuice, but they'd changed positions. Her face was pressed against the wall, Beetlejuice was behind her, and I couldn't tell where he was sticking it.

Hallow and I stepped back out into the dark. We found Celie at a corner table, sitting under a big photo of Tammy Wynette. She'd taken off the Bride of Frankenstein wig. Louis and Terry, two of our cooks comforted her. Louis had lost his blond Joe Exotic mullet, but Terry couldn't take off his because it was real. Celie dabbed her eyes with a napkin as Louis rubbed her back.

I approached her carefully. "How are you holding up, Celie?"

"I'm alright," she said.

I believed her. If Grady were indeed dead, she'd be more livid than anything. This was hard. I'd never been to a murder mystery dinner before let alone a surprise Halloween one. I tried my best to play along. "Do you know what happened?"

"They won't let me see the body," Celie snapped.

Terry chimed in, "They won't let anyone see it."

"Who found him?" I asked.

Louis answered me, "Earl. The big guy called them right away. He wouldn't let anyone in the freezer."

Earl was our one and only bouncer. "Why would he do that?"

Celie answered me, but she looked at Hallow like she just noticed him. "You wouldn't know it, but Grady was prospecting with that club, the Royal Bastards MC."

"Yeah, I had no idea." Ford had said something about it, but just last night. "Prospecting?"

"It's like a try out. He wanted to join them and had to prove himself." Celie swayed her head. "Grady done sold his soul to the devil. Earl was just doing what he was told since Grady belonged to that gang now." She paused. "Who's your friend?"

"Pardon me. Where are my manners? Celie this is Hallow. Hallow this is Celie."

As they said their nice to meet yous, I glanced around the bar. No one had moved from their spot, really. The bikers were still questioning folks. Dimple had left the stage for some Hot Chicken so Sheila, one of our barmaids dressed as a nurse, sang an eerie, incredibly quiet, acapella version of "Those Memories of You". No wonder we could hear ourselves think.

"You with them bikers?" Celie asked Hallow, pulling me back to the conversation.

"He's with me," I said to defend him.

Celie showed her teeth. "It's about time you found someone." She turned to Hallow. "You're one lucky guy."

I opened my mouth to tell her it wasn't like that but Hallow beat me to it. "Yeah. Eve is an angel."

"That's her name, Eve Angel. You take care of our girl." Celie ended the conversation, so I motioned for Hallow to follow me. Louis and Terry left to follow Dimple back to the stage. They started into "There Ain't No Good Chain Gang". With the makeshift band and the three of them, they sounded enough like the Highwaymen, making the place way too loud again.

Hallow caught my waist, surprising me.

Getting close, he whispered, "So, Eve is your real name. Eve Angel."

"I told you as much."

Hallow's arm twisted around me. We hugged up like Donette and I usually did, like we were about to slow dance. His tongue darted out and licked my earlobe. "An angel who fell from heaven meant only for me." His rough hands went places they weren't welcome. Not in public anyway.

Fluttering my eyes, I smiled. He couldn't see it. As much as I enjoyed his touch, I pressed his hands away. I

talked into his ear, "You're acting like a demon that crawled out of hell."

Hallow's hands returned but stilled on my hips. "I might just be. But you're a temptress like your namesake." He laid a kiss under my ear that made me quake. My body responded as I about melted onto the floor, but I freaked out. "Not here," I squeaked in his ear.

"Then where?"

"Nowhere."

"You know, if we're going to mingle, find out anything it's best folks think we're not strangers."

"Everyone here knows that I have no love life to speak of."

"How's that?"

"I leave alone every single night."

"Celie didn't seem to suspect anything."

"You're right." I locked arms with him. "Let's try to find the killer."

We headed back to the bar. Ford knew good and well I wasn't with anyone, but I was bound and determined to get this game over with.

Greta and Viv claimed they didn't know anything about Grady's murder. They had no suspicions either. I'd tried to act casual, but they didn't buy it. Ordinarily, I never asked anyone anything. I rarely made conversation.

"The bikers already asked us," Greta said.

Viv added, "If I knew, I'm not one to snitch."

Hallow spoke up, "I heard he's a biker now. He's bound to have enemies."

Viv took the bait, "If you only knew the half of it."

Hallow gave me a look, and I slid down the bar to talk to Ford and Jasper, but Jasper was gone. Ford pointed to the stage. Dimple and our head cooks had just finished singing together and were at a table drinking. Jasper belted out a cover of Colter Wall's "The Devil Wears a Shirt and Tie" as he strummed a guitar.

"I'm impressed."

"You're not the only one who can sing," Ford said under his breath. "You're just the only one Grady let's sing."

I filed that away to think about later. "Who do you think did it?"

Ford was more receptive and didn't bat an eye at Hallow being down the bar talking to his bartenders. I'd already gotten on to him earlier. "I couldn't tell you. He was

in the kitchen a lot tonight. Since he said he wasn't closing the kitchen early like we normally do. Louis couldn't handle it. The crowd. The extra orders. You know they ain't used to cooking past eleven. My team was taking care of the mob without Grady or Celie, so we didn't notice anything."

"Celie was in the kitchen too?"

"No. She says she was on the floor, but I didn't get any of her orders."

"I can't believe Grady's dead."

"Bound to happen since he's running with those thugs."

"What did they ask you?"

"Same shit you're asking. But they wanted to know if I liked Grady. I said, well enough. I mean, fuck. I didn't want to see him dead. I've worked here six years. He made me head bartender last year over Viv who's been here ten. But you know why."

"Yeah, her trouble with the law." Everyone knew Viv was on probation. She said it a million times a shift.

Ford crossed his arms. "See, not everyone working here are good people like me and you, Eve. Someone here is a murderer."

"You know I'm pretty new." Most of the time I felt like I was a new character on the tenth season of a show since Bootsies had been open eleven years. I hoped I wasn't a red shirt, that I wouldn't be killed off. I had never thought about it literally of course, until now. I just always thought someone might throw me under the bus, get me fired, or make me want to quit. Donette always had drama. But both Grady and Celie had taken a liking to me, so nobody bothered me.

Jasper returned limping to the bar when Hallow joined me.

"That sent chills down my spine," I said to Jasper.

He halfway smiled and said, "The inmates are running the asylum." Jasper pointed across the bar.

Jaylynn started our mechanical bull. Grady hadn't wanted it turned on til' it was fixed. The bull would run for a bit before it started smelling like something was burning. Dumb twats were going to burn the place down.

"Looks like I'll be introducing you to Taco," I told Hallow.

"Who?"

"Our bull. Come on."

Hand in hand, Hallow and I made our way to the pit around Taco where my coworkers gathered. I expected

more Elvis songs, but Dimple went with the Halloween theme and sang "Honky-Tonk Hell". It was appropriate.

On our way to Taco the urge hit me, hard. "Excuse me, I've got to go tinkle."

"All right, I'll meet you over at the bull." I left Hallow and darted straight toward the employee bathroom. Finding it occupied, I knocked on it. Silence followed. I relished in the calm of the break room a moment until I remembered my full bladder. It must've been the beer. Taking off my apron, I felt like I would burst. I laid my apron on the breakroom table and paced. After a good minute, I banged on the door. "Shake the dew off your lily and get out of there."

There was no answer. I left the back and went towards the regular bathrooms. Thankfully, the women's room didn't have a line. Unheard of for a Friday night. Still, I didn't like to use our public restroom. I glanced at myself in the mirror on the way to a stall. I was a sight. My face glistened with sweat and oil, in a day of hard work. My hair was a frightening mess. I couldn't decipher what Hallow saw in me. Then I peered down. I'd worn the wrong bra. My nipples were plum out, showing through my white sheath of a dress. I went into the stall and stuffed some toilet paper into my bra to hide my nips. After I did my business, I had to undo my bandage to wash my hands. The cut looked alright, so I decided to let it breathe. I ran my fingers through my hair to tame it. I squirted some more soap on my hands to give my face a once over. My makeup was gone anyhow. With a clean face, I felt a million times better but knew I could do better. I wet a paper towel and went over my armpits and crotch next. Who knew where the night would lead? I bit my lip thinking about Hallow and I, me against the wall like Donette had been. Seriously hot for him, I splashed some cold water on my face. Was Hallow the right dick? I laughed thinking how he was a detective, a dick. Maybe it was meant to be, me and him. Hallow and Eve on All Hallows' Eve. Nah. It'd make a hell of a story, but I didn't believe in that shit.

When I made my way back out to the bar, I got another douse of cold water. I discovered Hallow and his big black wings leaning against the pit, cozied up with the rest of the barmaids. Jaylynn rode Taco, and his eyes followed her back and forth. In her sexy cowgirl costume, her tits were practically bouncing out. Her tan thighs provocatively slid back and forth on the bull as she bounced. Hallow appreciated the show with a big smile on his face. Sure, she was a hoot and holler, but Jaylynn gave white trash a bad name, I'd heard anyway. Not only that, Hallow was being worshipped by all the girls and loved every minute of it.

I found Donette amongst them and our eyes met. I gave her a look that could kill. She left the harem to join me. God bless her. She looked like she'd been rode hard and put up wet. I'd seen it happen myself. She didn't have on a stitch of the red lipstick that matched her dress. Beetlejuice's face paint was all over her cleavage.

"Oh, I'm so sorry. Eve. I thought maybe your right dick had come along," she said, observing our coworkers trying to climb Hallow like a tree.

"Dick's right." I meant he's a jerk, but added, "He was a detective."

"Oh, wow. A real dick, in more ways than one. What a shame."

"It's a real shame," I said, agreeing with her. "Fucking twats."

Donette's eyes widened at my rare curse word. She handed me her drink, a jack and coke. "Can't blame the girls. I wouldn't throw him out of bed unless he was better on the floor," she said as I downed it.

The whiskey, even watered down in soda, burned my throat. "I really thought about getting some practice in, ya know?"

"Eve, were you going to let him pop your cherry?"

"I'd really thought about it, Donette. No way in hell now."

Dimple appeared beside me. "They tell me you're a singer," he said, sounding just like Elvis.

"Sometimes," I answered, knowing he was going to ask me to get on stage. The crowd was thin enough and after all, it was a party. And apparently, I no longer had a date. When I followed the Elvis look alike to the podium, I grabbed an abandoned beer on the way. I'd drank it by the time I stepped in front of the mike.

Dimple said, "I'm thinking Halloween. But I'm thinking blues. Nina Simone."

I completed his sentence, "I Put a Spell on You. Yeah, I can sing that."

Dimple got behind our upright bass and quickly directed the rest of the ragtag band to play the right chords. There were no saxophones, but two of our kitchen crew and one guest played guitar, keyboard and a fiddle. Closing my eyes, I started out strong. With alcohol calming my nerves, I opened my eyes. Hallow's big brown eyes glowered my way. As I belted out the ballad, I gave him the stink eye in return. The lyrics were way too appropriate for the moment, making me feel way too vulnerable, but I wouldn't tear my gaze from him. Peeling the girls off him, he started to come over to the stage, but the girls surrounded him again, blocking his way. Fuck, he could come to me if he really wanted to. Seeing the other barmaids hang on him, rage flowed through me. Hallow was mine. I let my fury come out in a melody and hit all the right notes.

Our eyes fixed, I sang to Hallow like he was the only man in the room. I felt every word deep in my soul. They were true. I didn't care about anything else. I belonged to him in this moment, tonight. When my song ended, there

was a round of applause. Instead of enjoying it, I bolted through the bar to hide in the back. Hallow followed me, shouting, but I couldn't hear him over Dimple who had started a jazzy rendition of "Blue Eyes Crying in the Rain". Fighting tears of my own, I rushed to the employee break room, back to the bathroom and tried the knob. It was still locked or was it. Twisting the knob, I shoved on the door, and it sprang open.

"Sorry," I said almost immediately. I shut the door quick. Dern, I'd done walked in on someone. Was that big Earl with his pants down?

Hallow reached me. "Eve, why did you run off?"

Blowing air out of my nose, I didn't answer him.

He trapped me against the door, his forehead to mine. "You got jealous?"

"Jealous of what?" I pouted.

"All the ladies crowding me."

"Crowding you? They looked like cats in heat rubbing against you."

"They were dancing to your beautiful song, your enchanting voice. I was stuck in the middle of it."

"They were like my Gran antiquing, after your junk. Looks like you were enjoying yourself, too."

"Just watching the show."

"Watching Jaylynn ride that bull, her titties almost falling out."

"I'd rather it be you riding the bull. Or riding me." His lips were so close to mine we could kiss.

My hands were flat on his warm chest. I could feel his heart beating hard under my flesh. "We just met."

"What's it matter?" His lips hovered over mine, his scruffy beard tickling me.

I moved my hands onto his shoulders to hold him back. "With all due respect, I'm not like Donette. I'm not that kind of girl."

I barely got out the last word.

Hallow's lips engulfed mine, lugging us into a sweltering kiss. His tongue worked its way down my throat as his rough beard scoured my chin. He tasted refreshingly new like the beer but sweeter. I had no complaints. My arms went around his thick neck as I enjoyed every minute of our kiss. His hand coiled under my skirt and into my panties before I could protest. Like lightning, his rough touch struck me. I'd not been touched in so long. Not by anyone but myself in way too long. My breath hastened as he found me more than aroused. Humming into our kiss, he seemed to like how soggy my bottoms were. Spry fingers danced against my delicate parts for just a moment. But

then Hallow removed his hand and slipped them up my dress to cup my breasts. I regretted the paper I'd shoved in my bra to hide my nipples. He soon remedied that by reaching behind me and undoing my bra to get to my skin. My naked flesh was his gift. Hallow didn't care to save the wrapping paper.

Never breaking our kiss, he had my bra off, on the floor, and my dress hiked up to my chin in no time. Our tongues fought as he fondled my breasts, squeezing my hardened nipples ever so gently. Ending our kiss, Hallow slipped off his wings and let them fall behind him. Our eyes met briefly. His were full of lust or was that mine reflecting? His hungry mouth hung open as he regarded my body, so I shut mine. Then he bent down to get a mouthful of titty while his hands tugged my drawers completely down. I stepped out of them. God love a duck, Hallow's head slid down my stomach, his mouth trailing leaving kisses. He stuck his face right in my coochie.

On his knees, his tongue darted out as his hands took my knees to spread my legs wide open. His warm tongue hit my clit, causing me to wobble on weak legs. As he licked, he steered my legs over his shoulders one by one. Lord have mercy. Hallow's mouth widened as he wolfed my whole pussy. He ate me like a pig eating sweet potato pie. Leaning against the door, I let my head fall back as he pleasured me. I held onto the hair on his head as he worked his tongue just right until I came. It hadn't taken long. I howled at the moon, like a loon. Removing my legs, Hallow came up my body and undid his belt.

I about died. "Now hold your horses," I panted out. I didn't know if I was ready for all that.

My words didn't stop Hallow from drawing out a massive dick. No, I wasn't ready for all that dick. His cock was glorious, just as gorgeous as the man, but was it the right dick? If not his who's? I wondered. What was I waiting for? His body pressed against mine, dick and all. Skin to skin, he felt so nice. Regardless, my nerves were tore up. Hallow took my uninjured hand and placed it on his thick rod. I couldn't wrap my fingers around it, not completely. Hot and hard in my hands, his cock throbbed. Hallow kissed my neck and rocked his hips gently making his dick slide in and out of my grip. My breathing heavy from just getting off, I quivered, thinking of his cock probing my insides. The thought both enticed and frightened me.

His hot breath tickled my ear. "Are you ready?"

"No," I puffed.

"Don't think you can handle this big dick?" Hallow purred.

"No. I ain't done this before," I whispered into his ear.

"You've got to be shitting me."

"Honest to God."

Unexpectedly, Hallow's finger slipped inside me.

Him poking me sent reminders of my climax through me. I squeezed his cock.

"Fuck, you're telling the truth," he groaned.

"Why would I lie?"

"To turn me on." He moved his hand more and really flipped my libido back on. "You've never done anything?" he asked, into my neck.

"I've had orgasms."

"You've never had anything inside you?"

"No. Not until just now."

"My finger is barely in. Not even a dildo?"

"No." Lord, this was embarrassing.

"Ever had a man eat your pussy before?"

"No," I said, blushing. "Not before you."

"Ever sucked a cock?"

"Kind of. I'm really inexperienced."

Hallow froze. "How old are you?"

My hand opened and his dick fell away. Lordy. We knew nothing about one another, and I'd been debating letting this man take my virginity. Here I was panties down and dress up in the employee break room, a half-naked man against me. Was I drunk? Surely not, although I'd downed that jack and coke moments ago and had a few beers tonight. Warm all over, my face felt hot, but I'd just had a terrific orgasm. Even under Hallow's spell, my head felt clear enough even though my nerves weren't quite as bad as usual. "I'm twenty but turning twenty-one in December," I answered him.

Hallow chuckled like that was a surprise. "At least you're legal." His hand moved again.

"Not to drink," I squeaked as he got a little rough.

Hallow slowed his finger again. "You're not drunk, are you?"

"No. I ain't," I said, but I knew that the alcohol had lifted some fear in me. "Are you? How old are you? How many sexual partners have you had?"

"No. I'm not drunk. Twenty-eight, and no one's ever asked me that before." His movements quickened, and I felt he was fucking me with his hand.

"That many? Well, I'm a not made it past third base girl."

"We can work our way up to a homerun."

I sputtered a laugh at that cheesy line.

Hallow beamed like he'd been trying to be funny. Now his tone turned more carnal. "Let's just say I'm experienced enough to give you the ride of your life. Taco has nothing on me."

"See, I'm afraid, I'm going to fall off the bull. That's if I get the nerve to jump on to begin with."

"I won't let you fall. I promise."

Hallow removed his finger from me, and I instantly missed it. He placed my hand on his dick again. Although my hand snaked down the length of it, and I envisioned doing so myself, I shuddered my head. "I don't think I can," I said with a pout.

Hallow caught my fat lip and sucked. We devoured each other, kissing again as his erection swayed into my hand. His mouth tasted salty now, like me down below, I supposed. Remembering his head between my legs turned me on even more. Thinking of the way he'd made me feel, returned the sensation. My desire, a ticking time bomb, I wanted another explosion. Hallow rammed his body hard against mine with the rhythm. The motion mimicked the act I'd witnessed earlier, Donette getting plowed against the wall. His thigh surged against my clit each time in cadence. "

I was about to give in but talked myself out of it. "I don't know that I can do this here. I don't know if I can go through with it at all."

"You're saving yourself for marriage or something?"

"No. I'm just chicken shit."

"So, let me get this straight. You want me, want me to fuck you, but you're too scared?"

"Yeah," I breathed, feeling how true that was.

"We can go to my place. I'll handcuff you to my bed so you can't stop me," Hallow said.

His words more than turned me on, but I asked, "You're into that?" Knowing he'd been a detective, I wondered if this was his kink.

"What? Restraining you and taking your virginity? Fuck. Sounds like a dream come true. Either that or I can fuck you up against this door right now. Just say the word."

At the mention of my back being against the door to the employee restroom, I thought about its occupant. Lord, what about Earl? He was trying to use the bathroom and could probably hear everything. What would he think of me?

Just as the thought hit my brain, Hallow's thrusts forced the door to fling open behind us. We tumbled into

the bathroom floor. Hallow amazingly caught the back of my head before it could hit the tile but landed on top of me, his dick dangerously close to my vag. Talk about a homerun. He almost slid home. His eyes widened, looking shocked and amused. The same feelings rolled through me, and I giggled. I turned my head expecting to see a surprised and bewildered Earl. Even an angry Earl, but Big Earl sat motionless on the commode, his pants around his ankles. His head hung, and dead eyes stared down at me.

CHAPTER 6

EVE

A blood-curdling scream escaped my lips as soon as I realized. At the same time, I saw blood speckled Earl's shirt and pants. My eyes followed the pattern to find the knife stuck in the back of his neck. In one swift motion, Hallow helped me to my feet. But I slipped away, grabbed my bra and panties, and ran to make some distance between me and the dead body. I slinked to the corner of the breakroom. Quick as lightning, I stepped into my drawers and hauled my dress down. Thankfully, I hadn't gotten a speck of blood on me. When I heard the heavy boots of the bikers coming our way, I tossed my bra into the open trash can. I stared at the row of lockers beside me, wanting to grab my phone and dial 911.

When the three bikers stepped through the door, they rushed to Hallow. I moved to help him, as if I could, but he held up his hand, telling me to stay back. The meanest looking one spun his head to examine me for a moment while Hallow relayed the news, that we'd just discovered Big Earl dead. Their leader locked the breakroom door.

Silently, I watched them pull Earl's body out of the bathroom and examine him. Hallow searched the shelves for something as I locked eyes with Earl. A biker bent and closed his eyes, releasing me. Hallow produced an old apron to partially cover the body, at least Earl's face.

"Fuck, this is getting to be a massacre. First Wolf and now Earl," their leader, Riff said. I'd just found their name tags. Clean shaven, he had dark and wavy, shoulder length hair, so nice, it'd make a woman envious.

"Are you talking about Grady?" I asked him.

"Yeah, Wolf's his road name." Slapping my hand over my mouth so I wouldn't scream again, I just realized Grady was indeed dead. Just like everyone had been saying all night. This was not a murder mystery dinner, like I'd thought. My boss had really been murdered. Had I been in denial? "Holy fuck," I murmured into my palm still trying to process the horrible fact.

"What were you two doing back here?" Riff leered at Hallow.

"Porking," another one, the real ugly one named Buzzard answered, smelling the air. "I smell a sweet wet cunt." Sickly thin, Buzzard's picture had to be in the dictionary beside the word meth-head.

The third one named Thorn, the ultra-muscular, black one, wore a cowboy hat with his leathers. He had an

impressive beard, but I didn't see any tattoos on his arms. He hadn't said anything but made up for it now. "We all going to get a turn, Hallow?"

Hallow took offence, punching him hard in the chest. Thorn just belted out laughing while the wheels spun in my head. All the men were cutting up like old friends.

Buzzard asked Hallow, "You going to bring this pretty filly back to Royal Road tonight? We're about to get out of here. Masquerade Orgy probably still going on."

Riff spoke, "Yeah, brother, we're going to cut and run before anyone else dies." He made a show of shivering. "I don't like all these people dropping dead unless I'm doing the killing. It being Halloween and all."

Hallow asked them, "You still don't know who killed Wolf?"

"We have our suspicions," Thorn said, while Riff answered, "No."

"Hallow," I said his name like they had, realizing these bikers were a bit too chummy with him. "You're one of them," I accused him as the thought cemented in my mind.

Hallow's lips disappeared.

Buzzard patting him on the back answered my question, "You didn't tell her you're a Royal Bastard?"

Thorn interrupted, "Hush your mouth, Buzz. It's supposed to be a secret."

"A secret?" My voice bore my anger.

Thorn continued, "Got this girl to fall in love with you yet, man?"

Riff hooted. "Oh man, sorry 'bout the cock block."

I started to stomp away. Hallow caught my upper arm and stopped me. I tore from his grip. "Get off me, you liar."

"Where do you think you're going?" Riff stepped in my way and lit a cigarette, blowing smoke in my face.

"You can't smoke in here. And I'm leaving."

"We've not questioned you yet. Sit down."

Hallow snatched me again by the arm and drug me into a chair at the break room table. Riff sat in front of me flanked by the other two. Hallow stood at my side, his hand on my shoulder like he'd make me stay put if I tried to stand up.

"You take orders from them?" I glared up and asked him.

"I do," he answered, his mouth tight like a little butthole. What an asshole!

Riff began his interrogation. "You fuckin' your boss?"

"Wha…no…" I choked out. "I don't mean to sound rude, God rest his soul, but Grady was old enough to be my dad."

"Everyone else seems to think you two were bumping uglies."

"Who?"

"I'll ask the questions," Riff said and puffed on his cancer stick.

I waved my hand in front of my nose. "Do you have to poison me while you do it?"

Hallow's hand squeezed my shoulder as a warning.

Riff ignored my comment about his smoking. "Everyone says Wolf had a crush on you. You know anything about that?"

"Well," I began and grimaced.

"So, you know?" Hallow spoke up at my side.

"Yeah, but…"

Riff went on, "They say he let you sing every night."

"He does. He did."

"Who else sings here every night besides the hired bands?" Riff asked.

"Grady and Celie."

"Him and his ex-wife?"

I nodded.

"They say you've not dated anyone in two years," Riff said, narrowing his eyes like he didn't believe it.

"That's true."

"Why is that? Pretty, young girl like you?"

Lifting my shoulder, I showed them my palms. I certainly wasn't about to tell them about my nerves. About my stage fright and date fright. I thought I'd been getting over it with Hallow. That ship had certainly sailed.

"Your friends assume it's because you're secretly seeing your boss."

"What?" I exclaimed and started to stand.

Hallow's nails dug into me as he held me down.

I hugged myself. "I ain't sleeping with Grady. I wasn't."

"You're in his phone as Eve Angel." Riff pulled out Grady's phone. I recognized it from the grey case with a Bootsies sticker on the back.

"That's really my name, not a term of endearment." I looked to Hallow for some help. "Tell them that's my name."

Hallow didn't say a word. Ass!

"The last text he sent you was a doozy. Dear Angel,"

"What in the Sam Hill? I didn't get no text like that."

Riff went on, "Last night you made me harder than... Well, I'm not sure I should go on. This is quite racy. Says he can't wait to bust your sweet cherry."

"What?" My voice cracked.

"Your text to him before that reads, I need you now. Did you send that text last night at three-thirty a.m.?"

I had to think for a moment. "Why yes, I did, but I didn't need him like that."

Hallow let go of my shoulder completely.

Talking a mile a minute, I relayed the story about almost being abducted last night and texting Grady when he didn't pick up his phone. "Then I called him again and he answered because I needed him to go check on Ford. Didn't Ford tell you all about this?"

Riff rocked his head. "Not a word."

"Ford said it was probably y'all who tried to kidnap me."

Riff smirked. "Sounds like something my boys would do. Didn't you see this girl last night Hallow?"

"Last night?" I echoed Riff, confused.

"Yeah, I saw her," Hallow answered.

I looked at him sideways, my brow creased.

Riff asked him, "You try and take her then?"

Hallow crossed his arms. "Nope."

Riff asked me, "Did you file a police report?"

"No."

"Hmm. That's curious." Riff tapped his finger on his chin.

"I was tired. Why are you asking me all these questions? You think I killed Grady?" I laughed. "That's crazy."

Riff sat way back and shook his head to free his thick hair from his neck. "As unlikely as it seems, your family history is mighty interesting."

"Who told you about that?"

"About your father? Your friend in the red says your dad spent some time in the nuthouse, and when he got out your mom was hacked to bits and thrown in the river."

Hearing it told like that made my stomach turn. Fucking Donette. How could she? I jutted my chin out trying not to cry.

"And that's not all she told me about him."

Figured. Taking a deep breath, I bleated out, "He didn't kill her. And what does it have to do with me?"

"Nuts don't fall too far from the tree. Hallow, you check her for tattoos?"

"She's clean," Hallow answered, and I never felt dirtier.

Hallow hadn't just been getting it on with me, he'd been searching my body. "I didn't kill Grady, I swear," I insisted.

Riff leaned in, "How did you hurt your hand?"

"Slicing limes."

Riff stood up. "With this knife?" He asked, slamming a knife on the table in front of me like it was the big reveal.

Jumping back, I could only assume the bloody knife came from Grady's murder. The fact Grady had actually been murdered sank to the pit of my stomach and made me tear up again. I wiped at my leaky eye and took a breath. Hallow's hand returned to my shoulder but not to hold me down. His caress was meant to comfort me. Composing myself I answered Riff, "Maybe. All of our knives look the same. There's an identical one in Earl over there."

Riff put his cigarette out on the side of the table. "We're done here. Hallow, you comin' home?"

"In a minute."

The bikers left Hallow and me alone. He took the seat in front of me.

Where would I begin? Angry, I had so many questions for Hallow. "You think I killed Grady?"

"No." His face contorting backed him up.

"Then why didn't you say anything?"

"Riff's just fucking with you. Fucking with me too. I might as well be probate. I'm a transfer."

His words meant nothing to me. Juddering, I held out my hands.

"I'm new. Transferred from another chapter of this club. I've got to watch my step. Riff's Road Captain, and I'm a peon."

"You're a biker. A Royal Bastard." Bastard was right. "Why didn't you tell me? Is it true?" I didn't finish, but I'd been talking about what his friend said, that he'd been here last night. That he'd seen me.

Hallow narrowed his eyes. "Yeah, you told me you didn't date nasty bikers, remember?"

I gasped. Hallow was the biker I bumped into last night. He'd trimmed his thick beard. Too many thoughts entered my head at once. Feelings of betrayal and mistrust overcame me. "That was your girlfriend who about attacked me?"

"Ex. And we were just friends."

"Fuck friends, I assume."

Hallow turned it on me. "That text from Wolf. What was all that about? Got him so hard..."

"Nothing. I don't know. I never received it."

"Where's your phone?" he demanded.

"In my locker like it's been all night. We're not allowed to keep them on us anymore. Grady's rules."

"You been in here to check it?"

"A few times."

"Let's see it."

"Okay," I said, shaking my neck with attitude. I had nothing to hide. I grabbed my apron off the table, always aware that my earnings were in it. I'd stuff it away, as well. Standing up, I walked to my locker, the third one from the right. They weren't numbered. Seizing the lock, getting ready to put my combination in, I found it undone. After my last break, in my haste to get back on the floor, I probably left it unlocked. Removing the bolt, I lifted the latch. I shoved my apron inside and retrieved my pocketbook, a simple, no-name brown leather clutch. Unzipping, I dug out my cell and handed it to Hallow who'd been on my heels.

He handed it back. "Passcode."

I typed in my numbers, and we looked at my phone together. Our heads bumped as I clicked on my texts, on Grady who was in my phone as Bossman.

"Bossman, eh?"

"He's my boss."

Hallow huffed.

"You jealous?" Then I huffed, cause Lord almighty. The man was dead. There was no reason to be jealous.

To my surprise, there sat Grady's suggestive text, about a mile long. Hallow and I skimmed it. His proposals were nasty, saying all he wanted to do to me. Some things I didn't know were possible or legal. At the bottom of the text the read receipt said, Read at 11:15pm. And it looked like I sent an eggplant emoji back at the same time. But I hadn't. "What in the... I didn't do this. At eleven fifteen, I was knee deep in orders. My locker was unlocked."

Hallow's features dissolved into a scowl. "What do you mean? You didn't say?"

"You were right here. I didn't put in my combination. I didn't think I had to say it. I didn't expect this. I didn't read his text or send the eggplant."

Hallow's nostrils flared, and his face reddened like he didn't believe me. That's when the lights flickered before going off completely.

I reached for him in the dark, finding his hand. "I promise I didn't send that."

His hand limp, he didn't respond.

The lights came back on.

Walking away, Hallow didn't say a word. For the first time I saw his back without his wings. A big three-piece biker patch tattoo covered most of it.

I shouted, "Why are you mad? You lied to me."

Following him out front, I discovered Elvis had left the stage. The bar sat eerily silent as a crowd huddled in the middle of the dance floor. Riff hollered for everyone to get back. The people parted and a biker laid on the ground. The one they'd left to guard the door laid in a pool of blood. Dimple checked his pulse, his face looking grim. I caught up to Hallow to peek around his bulky frame.

"Must've happened when the lights went out," he said loudly, addressing everyone.

"Now someone's picking us off," Greta screeched.

The crowd grew louder with folks complaining.

Celie announced, "I'm calling the cops."

"You do that, and you'll never know who really killed Grady," Riff warned her.

"Wait a minute? You called the bikers in?" Louis, our head cook accused her.

Everyone fell silent.

With a stern face, Celie admitted to it with a bob. "Someone here has killed the father of my children. I planned to find out who and have swift justice." The crowd grew loud again as we all realized she meant for the bikers to take care of the killer. Kill the killer, or whoever they thought was the killer. Celie put her hands on her hips and got loud. "But Earl is dead and." Everyone gasped, not

knowing this information before. Celie motioned to the dead biker on the floor, "I'm washing my hands of this."

Thorn confronted her. "Got real Royal blood on your hands now, bitch."

Dimple stepped between them, his large belly making Thorn take a step back.

Tugging on his arm, I asked Hallow, "He one of y'all, too?"

Hallow bowed an answer because he was engrossed in the scene.

Riff addressed Celie, "On behalf of Kingpin, we regret Wolf's untimely death. With him not being a patched member, yet we were about to let this be. Just for tonight. Not sure the killer's still here. Can't find a motive."

"A motive?" Celie shouted.

"Yeah, seems everyone loved Wolf around here. He was a great feller."

Celie broke loose of Elvis and beat on Riff's chest. "I know he was. He sure was until he started messing with the likes of you. He was killed because of you bikers." Celie finally showed her true colors. I knew she'd be mad as hell if Grady had truly been murdered.

I cried with her.

Riff caught her hands, ignoring her anger and turned to Hallow. "What do you think, detective?"

Hallow wrenched his neck, "I have my suspicions."

Buzzard sounded in, "I have my suspicions, too."

Thorn blurted out, "Me three."

Riff went on, "Now that our brother, Sadist is cold, we're done playing. Celie you best wait until we're gone to call the fuzz, or they'll be hell to pay."

Celie seemed resolved. She stopped fighting and signaled her agreement.

Riff addressed the crowd, "Goes for the lot of you. You don't want to be on the Royal Bastards' kill list, you never saw us." He placed his hand on Elvis's shoulder. "Brother, I know you've got your cage, get Sadist home."

Cage?

Dimple seemed reluctant. "I drove the Cadillac," he said, and I realized they were talking about a car.

Riff countered, "So? Wrap him up tight."

"I'm going to need some help dragging him out of here."

"Take whoever you need."

Dimple chose Ford to help him, grabbing his shirt collar. Ford had changed out of his sweatpants and Titan's jersey into a button up and jeans. Since he'd be dealing with a dead body, I bet he was glad not to get his precious jersey dirty.

Riff turned to the other bikers. "Boys, grab a suspect. Whoever you think killed our brothers, their accomplices. They can answer to Kingpin. We're getting out of here."

As soon as the words left Riff's lips, Thorn and Buzzard snatched me by either arm. "Hey! How the hell would I have killed him? I was in the back." Protesting, I searched for Hallow who had left me and grabbed a hold of poor Jasper by his shirt collar.

Jasper sputtered out, "I'm innocent, man."

His buddy Ford who was helping wrap up Sadist didn't come to either of our rescues, but Greta complained, "You need to leave poor Jasper alone. He's. He's special."

"No. I ain't," Jasper snapped.

Hallow jerked him forward. "He's too quiet. Got blood on his boot."

Realizing him and Buzzard picked the same person, Thorn let go of me quickly and seized Donette.

"Oh my God. Do I look like I could kill anyone?" Donette laughed.

Thorn explained, "This one's crazy enough."

Donette started repeating Beetlejuice again.

The guy in the striped suit stepped forward, his makeup smeared, and clothes disheveled. Thorn dared him with a crack of his neck. Beetlejuice skulked back, disappearing into the crowd. Donette crossed her arms, looking pissed. So much for an Omega male.

Riff took our cook Louis by the arm and drew his gun to keep his suspect still. He'd been the only one to do that. With a pistol to his head, Louis was as quiet as a mouse. Riff didn't tell us why he thought our cook had done it.

Buzzard barely held my arm as he explained, "She's the one who killed Wolf, I know it."

"I swear, I didn't," I called to everyone.

Buzzard told everyone, "They had something secret going on. Something sexual. She knows something at least."

"We did not," I said, eyeing Celie.

She puckered her lips and quivered in disgust, breaking my heart.

Searching for Hallow again, I watched in horror as he gagged Jasper with a bandana. He tore a mask off a nearby patron and put it on Jasper's head, a green alien mask. Buzzard followed suit and almost did the same to me. Automatically, I spun around and kneed the ugly guy in the balls and got loose. Just as quick, Hallow let go of Jasper to capture me in his arms.

"I've got her," he told his brothers as Jasper ran off.

With Buzzard bowled over, Thorn let go of Donette and went after Jasper.

Riff threw his keys to Hallow. "I'll be taking Louis in the cage. Get them two secured and go with Buzzard. Thorn can take care of the runaway."

Buzzard, recovered, came at me, his fists up.

Hallow dared him to mess with me. "I've got her. You're not going to lay a finger on her."

Buzzard snarled at me but bent and handed the bandana he'd planned to gag me with to Hallow. "You know the rules about uninvited guests."

Before I could argue or fight, Hallow twisted me around and tied the bandana around my mouth to muzzle me. Holding me motionless, he plucked a mask off the floor and jerked it over my head. All went dark until Hallow tugged the mask more and my eyes lined up with the holes. Thankfully, they weren't just slits. As I fought to breathe, he bound my hands in front of me with another bandana. I could only assume Donette met the same fate as Hallow heaved me through Bootsies, out the front door and situated me on the front of a motorcycle.

Hallow's voice came muffled through the mask that covered my ears. "I'm taking you home to Royal Road to see my boss, the President of the Royal Bastards MC. You behave and listen to me, and you might make it out of there alive." He climbed on behind me, held me with one arm tucked around my waist and started the engine. As the machine roared to life, real fear finally settled in. Hallow, as much as I'd wanted him earlier, was an outlaw, a criminal like these other bikers. He obviously followed their orders, even when it came to me.

Chapter 7

EVE

The wind on the ride through Nashville chilled me to the bone. After all, thanks to my romp with Hallow, I was only in a paper-thin white dress, wet panties with no bra. Oh, and a freaking Halloween mask on that obstructed my vision. I found I could breathe just fine if I calmed myself. At least it kept my face warm. I shivered so hard that when we stopped, I was relieved. That was until Hallow chatted up someone who sounded like they were unlocking a gate. Lord have mercy. We must've gotten to Royal Road. The whole ride I'd prayed Hallow would have mercy on me and not really take me to his President. How hard would it be to drop me off on the side of the road and say I got away?

Hallow eased me off the motorcycle and led me through a door. Just inside, I heard live music very much like at Bootsies. They were playing Halloween songs too, a rocking, "Werewolves of London" to be exact. We stopped. I couldn't see a thing through my mask but the glare of neon.

"Hallow, did you bring us a treat? You can put her with the other girls," a muffled voice came.

"No, Opry. We're here to see Kingpin."

"Party's still on."

"You seen Buzzard?"

"No, not unless he's masquerading as someone else." He sniggered. "Get it? Masquerading... fuck man. Who pissed in your helmet?"

"How about Thorn?"

"Not seen them since they left the party about Wolf. You hear what happened to him?"

"He's dead."

"And you think this pretty little thing killed him?"

"Where's Kingpin?"

"He's in the throne room."

The throne room?

Hallow carted me through a loud party, obviously dodging folks. Once we made it through and to another entrance, he stopped and scooped me up to carry me. From then on it felt like he was wading through a bog until he sat me on my feet on dry land.

"Riff said you were bringing me a treat," a man's deep voice rumbled. You could still hear the music from the front room albeit it was much quieter.

"Not a treat." Hallow cleared his throat. "A suspect in Wolf and Sadist's murder. But with all due respect, Pres., she's innocent."

"Not a treat, eh? Take off her mask."

Hallow carefully lifted the mask off my head, and I breathed heavily through my nose since my mouth was still restricted. Blinking, my eyes adjusted to the low light. Throne room was right. The biker before me perched on an honest to God throne draped in red velvet like he were the Queen of England. Kingpin, I presumed. Long dark hair, straight with plenty of volume and a substantial beard, black mascara and matching nails, the guy looked more rock than country. But it was Halloween after all.

Shirtless, the biker showed off a chest and two arms full of black tattoos, some nice and some not so hot. His abs were impressive and bare of ink or hair. Kingpin wore leather pants, period, and they were undone revealing a bare patch where a bush should be. Dangling down, his tattooed feet were on display, each toenail black. Beside them a woman laid with a feathery masquerade mask on and not a stitch more. Her long bleached blonde hair almost covered her breasts that defied gravity. Dern, her body was perfect, perfectly fake probably. Her tongue darted out, and I realized she'd been licking Kingpin's toes.

Eww.

Following her were more people on the ground. I twirled around to see lots of folks all over the floor, all naked and wearing masks of some sort whether it be a fancy dress or a scary Halloween one. Their bodies tangled, connecting wherever they fit to another. Looked like a big game of naked twister to me. Glancing at the mask in Hallow's hand, the one that had been on me, I saw for the first time it was a tiger mask.

Kingpin searched me up and down. His dark eyes heavy with lust fluttered all over me. He addressed Hallow, "Looks like a treat to me."

"Not one that I can share."

Kingpin raised his eyebrows at that. "Welcome to Royal Road's Masquerade Orgy..."

"Eve," Hallow finished for him.

I couldn't reply because of the gag.

"Yes, Eve. Get rid of that frock and turn her around."

Shocking the hell out of me, Hallow did just as his President said, snatching my dress off over my head, exposing my bare body to Kingpin. My white dress pooled at my tied hands, hanging down like a ghost.

"I need to see all of her," Kingpin complained.

I jumped sideways this time but Hallow quickly righted me and hauled down my panties. He spun me again. "I've checked every inch, no tattoos."

"Yet, her dad is supposedly the notorious Fighting Cock."

"That's what her friend told Riff, but she never mentioned him to me."

"Raise your arms," Kingpin commanded. "Spread them."

In my defense, I hadn't known Hallow was even a biker. He lied to me. Muzzled, I couldn't defend myself. At the mention of my dad, I gladly showed him my body. Proof that I wasn't affiliated to his old biker gang. My parents had been divorced for as long as I could remember, and my mom kept me far away from any bikers. Dad was never around while I was growing up but was retired now. That's how he put it. He claimed to have left the club when my mom was murdered, but there was more to it. People claimed the biker gang somehow kept him from being convicted of killing my mom. A troubled man with more demons than hell, he was no angel. However, I never believed he killed my mom. Not for one second. The State of Arkansas agreed with me.

"What about her feet?" Kingpin asked.

Since I was already naked, I stepped out of my white flats. Any other night I'd have on my Cowboy boots. I wiggled my toes.

"Let's see the bottoms," Kingpin demanded.

Hallow spun me and brought up each foot.

"Where's her friend?" Kingpin asked. "Was she the other girl? The one Buzzard lost?"

Donette had gotten away. Good for her. I was still mad that she mentioned anything about my dad to these bikers. I'd sworn her to secrecy.

"I don't think she's involved either. Thorn's bringing in my suspect soon. Buzzard suspected Eve. He's wrong. Eve's innocent."

"How so?"

"Grady…" Hallow began.

Kingpin stopped him "We don't use our real names around here. Would you like me to use yours? Wolf was only probate but show him some respect, man's cold."

"Wolf," Hallow corrected himself. "He went to help Eve when someone tried to take her last night, abduct her from a parking garage on Church Street. She'd left the scene, so Wolf was really helping their friend Ford who had been knocked out. Ford had been walking Eve to her car."

"What a gentleman," Kingpin commented.

"Wolf told Ford he almost caught the guy, almost hit him with his car. Told him that last night. Then this Jasper guy comes in to work limping, says he's been run over. If Wolf figured out that it was Jasper who tried to abduct Eve, there's your motive. Jasper slit Wolf's throat in the walk-in freezer with a chef's knife."

Jasper? Wait, that didn't make any sense. If Wolf, I mean Grady told Ford he about ran over the guy who tried to abduct me last night, told him about that last night, that was before I saw Ford and Jasper today. So why didn't Ford say something to me earlier when Jasper came in Bootsies limping? When had Hallow even talked to Ford about it? He hadn't mentioned it to me. Ford hadn't said anything to the other bikers. I'd asked them when they questioned me right before this mess. I made all kinds of noise into the gag wanting to ask Hallow when Ford told him about Jasper and tell him about Ford's omission. I also thought about Ford's change of clothes. Bouncing up and down, I tried, but Hallow and Kingpin completely ignored me.

Lordalmighty. The awful fact struck me and made me still. If Jasper tried to take me, Ford had to have been in on it. I remembered him practically shouting through the parking garage, announcing our arrival before someone struck him in the back of the head and came at me. Nevertheless, I hadn't suspected anything amiss until now. With Ford's change of clothes, I settled on him as my suspect. That boy didn't give a flip about what he wore and wouldn't have changed but to cover up a murder.

"I wanted the girl here anyway because of her connections. Buzzard had been following my orders. Thorn's bringing in this Jasper?" Kingpin asked, drumming his fingers together.

"Yeah, he should be. If he can catch him. Squirrely little fucker ran off."

"You think he killed Sadist, too?"

"Why wouldn't he? He already killed his boss."

Kingpin bit his fist. "Sadist, he was my favorite. Sadistic bastard." He bowed his head and Hallow followed suit. Were we having a moment of silence? Kingpin peered up and rubbed his beard, thinking before he said, "Who is going to run our BDSM club now? Anyone tied to Sadist's death will suffer greatly. I'll have to question Jasper myself. Your girl here and the others too, but tomorrow. This shit's not going to ruin Halloween." He waved us off, trying to look around us at the orgy.

Hallow bowed a bit and started to drag me away, but Kingpin stopped him. "Wait. About you not bringing a treat. Not sharing..."

"Sir, I claim this one."

Kingpin's face lit up, and his eyes widened. "Is that so? So soon after..." He snapped his fingers.

Hallow helped him, "Steph."

"Steph? Yeah, that firecracker. I don't know if I believe it. Why are you keeping this girl from me?"

"I ain't," Hallow began.

Kingpin wasn't listening. "I know the good cop in you would hate to think, I'd take advantage of this sweet girl, but I promise you, that won't be the case. If I find out she's really the daughter of Fighting Cock, I won't just fuck her myself, we will all get a turn to use her before I send her back to her pop in little pieces. I'm certain the biker you are now knows as much."

"She's mine," Hallow growled, pulling me to his side like an animal.

Kingpin bowed to him a bit. "Are you sure you want to claim her? She's connected to a rival gang, tattoo or not. I ran the Asphalt Gods out of Tennessee. You want to give them a reason to try me again?"

Out of nowhere a woman appeared beside Kingpin wearing nothing but a pumpkin mask. That and her boob-o-lanterns. Each tit had an orange jack-o-lantern painted on. I had no idea where she'd been hiding the pistol, she pointed at Hallow.

Hallow stood his ground until she pointed it at me. He relented, "No, sir. I mean, yes, I claim her. No. I don't want no trouble."

"For the last time detective, do not call me Sir. It's Pres." Kingpin pulled up a knee and wiggled his toes. "I forgot you're a smart one. Did you know the Arkansas Gods' killed Leviathan's sister? Leviathan's our Enforcer but you may have not met him, yet. Not enough action for him here sometimes that he needs to go clean up messes elsewhere. Damn, he's a monster. The only thing that would save sweet Eve here from his... our wrath would be a property patch. I don't see one, but since you're fixing to..."

"Yeah, I'm fixing to, real soon."

"I'll want to see it." He pointed to my body. "I want it big on her shoulder and going up her neck."

"But shouldn't she get a say?" Hallow started.

Kingpin snorted. "A say? I suspect you won't want any trouble with your past. I know why you came to Nashville. You want to disappear. Being infamous isn't for everyone."

"It's worked out for you. Pres. But, no, I don't want it."

"You and I are much the same, both accused of a crime we didn't commit. Only difference is you got off

because you were the cop." Kingpin's crooked smile proved he really didn't like law enforcement.

"I shouldn't have gotten off, Pres."

"Then the life as a criminal, is this your punishment?" Kingpin lifted a shoulder. "You've been nothing but a loyal soldier since you got here. To be honest, I love what you're doing here right now." He motioned to the whole of us. "Lying to me to save this girl. But I won't be made a fool. I expect to see that you claim her and soon. I'm sure Blitz has an opening. Nothing he loves better than virgin skin."

"Yes, Pres. Within the week." Hallow regarded me for the first time since we'd gotten here, his eyes pleading with me. "Right, Eve."

Understanding the gravity of the situation, I nodded.

"We best be off," Hallow tried again.

"No. It's All Hallows' Eve..." Kingpin paused and grinned big. "Hallow's Eve." With his fingers splayed, he motioned between the two of us. "How fitting. I want you two to join my party. You can give me a real visual treat."

"Okay," Hallow said and went to remove my gag.

"No. Leave it. I like her like this. A woman always seems so innocent until she parts her lips. And put your masks on."

"I don't have a mask," Hallow told him.

Kingpin reached down and plucked a mask off the floor and threw it at Hallow. "Mask up and strip down, boy. This your first masquerade orgy or something?"

The woman at Kingpin's feet laughed, and he caressed her face. The woman beside him waved her gun, warning Hallow to do as he's told.

Hallow looked at me again, his lips forming a straight line.

Kingpin huffed, "What are you waiting for? You never earned that backpack here. I'll strip you of that one."

The look in Hallow's eyes told me he was sorry for what he was about to do. Obeying his President, he put on the mask, a white horse mask but a horn protruded from his head. No horse, it was a flipping unicorn.

"Hallow, you best fuck her brains out for me, or I'll do it myself," Kingpin warned.

Fuck my brains out? Right here at this Halloween orgy in front of everyone?

Hallow in the unicorn mask, but already topless, undid his big belt buckle and dropped his pants to the ground. I already knew he'd gone commando but was surprised his dick hung flaccid. I guess fucking me against

my will in the middle of an orgy didn't turn him on. A piece of me felt insulted, but I quickly came to my senses.

Kingpin noticed his limp dick, too. "Memphis, take care of that utter embarrassment."

Hallow protested by raising his hand, but the blonde crawled over and took his dick into her mouth. I couldn't watch. Gagged, I sure as hell couldn't do anything about it myself. I stared out into the orgy before us. How were they all still fucking? At least it was darkish out there.

Kingpin spoke again, "And Hallow, I want to see blood running down her creamy white thighs."

"What?" Hallow's voice echoed.

Kingpin winked at me. "Riff done told me she's a virgin."

I was going to kill Donette. Hallow's President already knew everything about me before we got here.

Before I knew it, Hallow put the tiger mask back over my head, took me by the balled-up dress at my wrist and led me down the stairs. At the bottom of them, he picked me up. He strode through the people all humping each other until we got to an opening. Placing me on my feet, Hallow took the dress and tore until it came off my wrists. He laid the dress out on the soft shag carpet.

I imagined he'd sit down and bring me on top of him, like I noticed a lot of couples were positioned, but Hallow laid me down on the dress. Good thinking. Who knew what grossness lived in the carpet? He steered my bound arms up and over my head. His nude body coated mine, and I could feel his erection hard against my thigh. Memphis had done an excellent job. Thinking of it made me fifty shades of jealous.

Holding himself over me, Hallow cocooned me from the others who wanted to reach out and touch my skin. Every once and a while someone got through and rubbed my boob as Hallow's free hand roamed all over me. In the mask, he wouldn't be using his mouth. Hallow's fingers drummed on my clit, before a finger slipped inside of me.

Oh. I gasped. Was this really happening? Memories of him eating my pussy earlier surfaced and helped calm my nerves. Hallow had made me feel amazing then. That was before we discovered Earl dead. I banished all the dead bodies out of my mind and focused on how I'd felt with Hallow in the breakroom. I let my jealousy toward the blonde who'd just had her mouth wrapped around Hallow's dick fuel my resolve. I never imagined I'd be losing my virginity like this, forced to in the middle of a Halloween orgy just because of my dad's poor life choices, but I could do worse than Hallow. I reasoned, if it'd not been him that brought me in to see Kingpin, I could've been gang raped and sent back to Arkansas as mincemeat. And if Donette hadn't opened her damned mouth about my dad none of

this would be happening. I was going to kill her for telling my business. If these bikers hadn't known I was a virgin, Hallow could've just pretended. Though, I didn't know if he would've even thought of that since I couldn't very well suggest it.

Why did he bring me here in the first place? Hallow worked his fingers gently through my wet pussy and wiped the question out of my mind. Yes, most of me wanted this. What a perfect way to just get losing my virginity over with. My mouth bound, I couldn't argue and stop him. Hallow had no choice, evidently. I ignored the part of me that whimpered for what ifs. As I convinced myself of the inevitability of the situation, my eyes closed in the mask as I imagined us anywhere but here. Did it matter if we were in the middle of a bunch of people? It was dark, and I doubted these strangers would remember anything in the morning. To them we were just a unicorn and tiger getting it on. With his hot skin pressed against mine and his fingers stroking my clit, soon Hallow made the people in the room completely disappear. A craving for him swallowed me whole. Desperately, I wanted him to do just as Kingpin said, fuck my brains out. My breathing quickened as I waited for Hallow to replace his fingers with something much larger, to break through and claim me like he said he would. One long finger turned to two and finally slipped in me.

Oh. Lordy.

Hallow only got rougher with his hand. Forcefully fucking me with two fingers, he went further inside of me than anything had before. There was no reason to be so rough or was there? It dawned on me he was trying to make me bleed without taking my virginity. How sweet of him. My body responded as I opened my legs and actually let myself really get into it. No reason not to enjoy it. But suddenly Hallow stilled. His fingers slipped away. I watched him out of the eye holes. He heaved up his mask to look down before he put the mask back on.

Just as suddenly, the fleshy head of his cock jutted against my clit. Without warning, in one big motion his dick broke inside me. Hard. I cried out into the bandana. Hallow shoved again, and I bit down as his dick actually ripped inside of me, all the way in. Drawing up my knees, I tried to ease the pain. I had no idea it was going to hurt so bad. Hallow didn't wait, he secured me by my shoulders and became a machine, hammering my insides. After that, a blur of pain translating to ecstasy took over. Hallow filled me full of dick while his hands were all over me. Then I realized, it wasn't all his hands, but I was too far gone to care about who reached in to cop a feel. My body belonged to the man tearing up my pussy. My brains weren't just fucked out, they shot out of my skull, hit the wall, slid down and landed on the floor in a gooey, gory mess. I'd thought I'd had orgasms before, but they didn't compare to the swell that rushed through me now. Eventually, my fucked-out brain exploded and landed in bits all over the crowd. I tried to see Hallow out the holes of the mask. The sight of

the unicorn head jerking above me crowded my vision. Hallow came too as he towed his big dick out of me. I felt a warm rush of liquid on my belly. The echoes of satisfaction consumed me, and I drifted in a river of serenity. But then Kingpin came into view, capsizing my boat of bliss. The fucker stood above us, watching. How long had he been there? When he walked off, Hallow took off his mask and mine. Taking down the gag, he asked me, "Are you okay?"

Completely weakened, I simpered. I was too pleased and winded to say a word. Hallow wrapped the dress around me and carried me out of the throne room. A live band still played although it had to be well past three a.m. now. A metal version of "The Time Warp" flooded the massive building. As we passed through the front room again, I saw it for the first time. The ceiling wrapped with fake cobwebs and big plastic spiders, as I let my head fall back. After all, I was still under the spell of some good dick. The colorful neon lights mimicked those of Broadway and lit up the webs. Straightening my neck, I found folks were dressed up much like at Bootsies but on a much larger scale, like Hallow's costume had been larger than life. But bikers in their leathers dotted the crowd. There was a stage for the band flanked by two stages for strippers. Nude women bobbed for apples on stage while more spun on poles in nothing but hats. A few wore cowboy hats, but a couple danced in pointy witch hats. Hallow strutted by buck naked but no one seemed to mind. A few women made catcalls at him when they pulled themselves from their gambling to notice. They weren't just playing poker like I saw Grady do in the back room at Bootsies a few nights, this was organized with women in skimpy uniforms running the tables.

"You hungry?" Hallow asked as we passed what looked like an all you could eat buffet.

I eyed all the food salivating before I noticed a toe. A woman laid out on the buffet table covered in Halloween candy. A couple of bikers ate smarties off her breasts as she cackled.

"No," I answered weakly. I found my voice though I was still out of breath. "Hallow, Ford."

"Ford?"

"Ford is the killer."

"How so?"

There wasn't time to explain. "He is. Trust me."

"Then my brothers, Dimple and Riff are in danger."

"Yeah, I guess so." Donette, Celie, everyone else was in danger too if they put two and two together.

Hallow turned to carry me up the stairs.

"Where are we going?"

"We were going back to my room for some privacy, I'm not finished with you, but now, I have to warn my brothers."

"You live up here?" We reached the top of the stairs.

"Only temporarily. I told you I'm new."

Hallow unlocked the door to reveal a room with two queen beds situated like a hotel. "I have a roommate, Thorn. You met him. He's rarely here."

I nodded as he sat me down to my feet and untied my hands. Holding my dress out in front of me, I studied the rips. There was no way I'd be able to wear it.

Hallow quickly dressed in jeans, a plain black t-shirt and his leather motorcycle vest. And voilà. He looked exactly like the biker who I bumped into at Bootsies the night before. Sexy AF. Go figure. I'd been so upset when I found out he omitted the fact we'd met before and that he was a biker, but now I blamed myself. How could I miss this? I blamed work in general. I saw so many faces. But none were as hot as Hallow. I'd not given him much thought before, but not only had I been working, I'd been threatened by his ex. Speaking of which, he handed me some jeans, a t-shirt and some canvas shoes. "Steph left some things here. They might fit. I figure you don't want her underwear."

"You figure right." Naked as the day I was born, I took the clothes. They were clean and folded and that was good enough for me.

"You might want to jump in the shower while I make some phone calls."

As he'd said it, I'd been stepping into the pants and saw the blood streaking my thighs. My stomach felt sticky too. I took his advice and found the bathroom while he talked into a landline. He didn't have his cell. Everything on him, he'd left in that throne room. I didn't want to go back there. My phone laid in the break room at Bootsies. My locker with my purse and apron in it was open too. I'd have to replace my debit card for sure. I had no idea what time it was, but my Gran wouldn't miss me until she woke like clockwork at seven a.m. Pleased it was clean, I found everything I needed fairly easily in the small bathroom except shampoo and conditioner. I took a quick shower using the men's body wash for everything. Relaxing under the spray, I thought about Kingpin saying I'd have to get a big tattoo up my neck. Over my dead body. How the hell would I become a famous country singer with a neck tattoo? As I washed my delicate parts, they throbbed with the reminder of Hallow taking my virginity. The ache felt nice. It'd been a long time coming. I fought back any regrets. As I toweled off, my mind was still on what had happened in the throne room. I might've not realized the gravity of the situation early on, but I was no dummy. Hallow had saved me from a worse fate. And like Grady had said, I needed to

get laid. Life was too short. Grady, he was dead and gone. The waterworks started. That's when Hallow decided to come into the bathroom.

"Don't you knock?" I sobbed out.

He captured me in his arms and held me to him. I cried for a good five minutes, getting his shirt all wet. "Eve, I'm so sorry. I would've never... If you really are Fighting Cock's daughter..."

"What? Are your friends going to kill me?"

"No. But we need to keep you away from Leviathan."

"Y'all don't have to worry about me. I'll never fool with bikers ever again." I dried my eyes on the towel.

Hallow took my shoulders and bent to look at me. "It's not that simple, Eve. I've told my president you're my girl and now you are, like it or not."

"Just like you fucked me against my will, right?"

Hallow took offense to that even though he'd just been apologizing. "You'll get a tattoo. Pretty simple, and tattoos can be removed now."

"I ain't getting no tattoo."

"Okay, then, but my ass is on the line now. I saved your hide back there."

"Is that all you have to say to me after what just happened?"

Hallow steered his eyes away. "Get dressed. I can't get ahold of Dimple or Riff. They're probably out at the pig farm disposing of Sadist."

"Disposing of him?"

"Burying him. He's dead."

"Don't he have family that'll miss him."

"Doesn't matter if he does. You never saw him, you hear?"

Dropping the towel, I stepped into the jeans and tugged on the shirt in front of him. Steph's shoes were a bit too big, so I tied them extra tight. "What about Ford? Y'all going to kill him for what he did to Grady?" I didn't mention the fact that he and Jasper tried to kidnap me. I didn't want to think about what they had planned to do with me.

"Yeah, we'll kill him, but Kingpin wants to talk to him first. I do too. I want to know what him and his friend planned to do to you and how many other girls they've lifted from Bootsies."

"What?"

"Asking around, one thing everyone agreed on was that turnover was mighty high. Celie said the other bars didn't have that much of a problem. She assumed someone working with you was harassing the girls and they weren't reporting it. She suspected Louis because of his criminal past."

"I didn't know he had one."

"Just possession, and I've known cops to plant drugs in cars, apartments."

"Why...?"

"Why did I quit the force? Made detective in Columbus, Ohio and at my age, that was something. You and I have something in common. When I was thirteen, my parents were murdered, both of them. The killer was never found. My uncle and aunt raised me after that. I spent so much time wanting to avenge my parents' death, but no one knew who killed them. I decided to become a detective and find out. The goal kept me on the straight and narrow path in Cleveland when all my friends turned to drugs or crime. Went to OSU, got a degree and joined the force. Took the exam after three years. Then, I messed up. A guy ran a red light, that's all. That shit was below my pay grade, even. Well, I didn't pull the trigger, but my partner did. Shot right into the cabin of the car, three times."

"For running a red light?"

"Jerry said our perp looked a lot like someone who held up a bank the week before. And that he had a gun. It was late at night. I didn't see one. We didn't find one."

"I'm sure that kind of thing happens lots with police, right? You're just doing your job and shit happens."

"Too often. Our suspect was black. He had two kids in his car, two young boys. We killed a man for running a red light. And I could've stopped it."

"How?"

"I don't know, but I got a bad feeling when Jerry walked up to that window. He was already on edge."

"Why didn't you stop him?"

"I was green, just made detective and just following orders. Jerry was my mentor... Just like I followed orders tonight." Hallow punched the wall in the bathroom door, leaving a dent behind. Like he was far away, he didn't stop there. He pounded a few more times, widening the hole.

A bit frightened, I carefully touched his shoulder. "Hey, obviously, you had to, right? I sure as hell didn't want to be raped and chopped into bits."

Hallow seemed to snap back to reality. He rubbed his fist. "Here, yeah. One wrong move, and Kingpin will send me to the pig farm and grind me into sausage. I don't care about that, but what he said they'll do to you, he wasn't

kidding. Leviathan, I know him. He's out for blood and anyone with a connection to the bikers who killed his sister will do."

"You weren't kidding about your friends being assholes."

"We have a code. But back in Columbus, I could've… I could've done something. I had a goddamned gun in my hand."

"What were you supposed to do? Shoot your partner?"

"We're trained to deescalate. But fuck, nothing had happened. Afterwards, I defended Jerry, my partner. I backed him up during the trial that was broadcast all over. Did you see it?"

"No."

"You're young. It was a few years ago. All we got was a smack on the wrist. Come to find out, after we were suspended with pay, my partner's racists internet posts surfaced." Hallow hung his head. "I don't know if that was why Jerry did it, it was dark and he said the man pulled a gun, but you can imagine the backlash. I fled the media circus and found myself in bum fuck nowhere, West Virginia without a pot to piss in. An old family friend gave me a job, and I started doing work for the Royal Bastards MC over in Charleston. I bought a motorcycle and finally became one of them. Wasn't too long before word had traveled down from Ohio about me. Not only am I known as a racist cop, but I'm also hated by the police for cutting and running. It's a no-win situation."

"If you don't want to be known as a bad guy or a racist why become a biker?"

"It's not about that anymore. I'm no one now. How low can I go? How far can I fall? I'm hollow inside." Hallow fell silent. "And how are the Royal Bastard's racist? What about Thorn? Wolf? There's all kinds of..."

"Grady?"

"His kids are black."

"I guess so." Celie's black so that'd make them black and white. "My dad was a biker, and he's a racist son of a bitch. Well, my Gran's not a bitch all the time, but you get my meaning."

"That's Arkansas for you. Nashville's no Cleveland but not as backwards."

I took offense to that. I wasn't backwards. I said as much.

Hallow replied, "Not you. I didn't mean..."

"You ever find out who killed your parents?"

"No. It was random so I probably never will. Your dad really Fighting Cock?"

"Was. Not anymore. Guess he got the name from fighting cocks. His side of the family raised the roosters. My Gran still has some laying hens up in Cottontown."

"They really fought chickens?"

"No. Not chickens. Cocks, yeah. No cock fighting in Ohio?"

"Oh, there is. I've heard. You have family here in Tennessee?"

"Yeah, my Gran. My dad's mom." I didn't say what I suddenly thought. Gran was in danger from this club, too. "My mom was an Angel from Boston. That was her last name, and that's why it's my middle name. She worked two jobs not counting church choir lead. She wanted to be a singer, but Henry Newberry saddled her with two kids and no help. See, my dad wasn't around when I was growing up. After my mom died when I was fourteen, he took us in but spent his time scaring guys away from me, laying out drunk and taking credit for every good thing my mom taught my brother and me. I left home as soon as I could, without his permission. No wonder dad didn't want me coming to Tennessee. At least now I know why he's not come after me. I shouldn't be in danger over a man who everyone thinks killed my mom."

"Did he do it?"

"Until now, I didn't think so. The papers went on about the backwoods biker and his hifalutin ex-wife from Boston. My mother's well-to-do family disowned her when she married my dad. And they didn't forgive her when she divorced him soon after. To be honest, I thought my dad liked to ride motorcycles and drink whiskey and that was all. I never believed all the tales about bikers being criminals. Any biker I ever encountered in Arkansas seemed nice enough and any claiming to know my dad was super polite to me. But hearing all this crap about his club killing people, Kingpin saying he'll cut me into pieces, I don't know anymore."

"Makes sense that bikers affiliated with your father would be nice to you and others wouldn't want to cause any trouble with you either."

"Never thought of it that way. Like I told you, my dad's retired now."

"Eve, once a club member, always a club member."

"Just being a biker doesn't mean he murdered my mom."

"Speaking of murderers, I'd like to get to Ford before he strikes again."

I agreed.

"Normally, I wouldn't take you within fifty miles of trouble, but I don't think you'll be safe here."

"Good. Cause I'm coming?" If Ford tried to kidnap me and killed my boss, I had a thing or two to say to him.

Hallow handed me a gun. "You know how to use one, right?"

Staring blankly at it, I said, "I might be from Arkansas, but I don't hunt or anything. I have no earthly idea."

Swinging around me, he circled me in his arms, bringing the pistol in my hands up between his. He drew one of my arms back tight to my body. "Keep this arm tucked in close, so you don't miss your target. Here's the safety. Keep it on. Here's the trigger. Don't shoot me." Taking the weapon, he ran it down my body to tuck it in my pants. "Not sure where you want to put this."

Not comfortable with a loaded weapon stuck down my denim, I asked, "Do you have a jacket I can borrow?"

"Nothing that wouldn't swallow you up. Here." Hallow left me to open the closet. Inside weapons neatly lined the shelves. Where did he keep his clothes? He came at me with a shoulder holster and helped strap it over my t-shirt. The gun tucked in under my left arm. Then he held up an oversized tracksuit jacket for me to slip into.

After I zipped it, I pushed up the sleeves, but it still fit me like a dress.

"Oh, and you're going to need this." He handed me a black helmet. Even though my hair was still wet, I situated it on my head and buckled the strap.

Hallow locked up the room and took me by the hand. He led me down the stairs and out a different direction that avoided the bar to a row of motorcycles. This time I climbed on back and wrapped my arms around him. When the motorcycle rumbled, I felt the first rain drop.

CHAPTER 8

HALLOW

When Buzzard chose Eve as a suspect, I knew I had to take her to Kingpin myself to clear her name. After all, the stinky bastard whispered to me in the breakroom that he thought she was Fighting Cocks daughter.

"Who's that?" I asked him.

"Arkansas God." That was all he had to say.

There wasn't anyone in the club that didn't know about our feud with the Asphalt Gods' MC or that the Tennessee Gods strung our Enforcer's sister up a telephone pole. They fucking crucified her, nailed her to the damned thing. Fucking gruesome shit. Leviathan wasn't our Enforcer back then, and I'd just joined the Charleston Chapter of the Royal Bastards MC as probate and missed all the action. So, I only heard tale of how Kingpin ran them out of the Volunteer state. Many of those bikers he ran out ended up in their Arkansas chapter. And Fighting Cock, I'd never heard of him but just being one of the Asphalt Gods put his daughter in danger.

The whole time Riff questioned Eve, I couldn't worry about her anger at finding out I was a biker. My mind raced, searching for a solution to our real problem. If Leviathan found out about her, he would no doubt kill her. Riff our Road Captain was one of the meanest sons of bitches I'd ever met who could also keep his cool. I thought being in Music City, with his long hair, the name Riff would have something to do with guitars, but I'd been wrong. Riff, short for Riffratt was born bad, he claimed. Yes, it's Riffratt not riff-raff, because he was a biker brat, or rather a biker rat, like they liked to call their boys. His late father had been Vice President of Smokey Rollers MC over in Sevierville back in the seventies. To Riff, being an outlaw was not just an occupation but a legacy. The man was serious about moving up the ladder. Kingpin kept him close because we all knew Riff wanted to rule.

My roommate Thorn was the biggest of the bunch. Kingpin, knowing my past, that I'm mistaken as my partner, the police officer who senselessly killed an innocent black man, thought sticking me with one of our few black members would be hilarious. Being ex-military though he didn't like to talk about it, Thorn and I got along well. He'd killed more innocent black and brown people than a white boy like me while he was overseas, he liked to joke. We also got along when it came to tidiness. His bed was always made before I woke up. Not a tattoo on him other than his backpack, he got up early to run before he hit the gym. Like me, he didn't touch the illegal drugs floating around the club and preferred to get drunk to party. We both took care

of our demons by working out or beating someone to a pulp. Unlike me, he was all country, wearing a cowboy hat most of the time. Other than that, Thorn and I knew little about each other. We certainly weren't up late at night chatting.

The direct opposite of Thorn, bald, toothpick of a man, Buzzard had to be the whitest man on earth. He was pushing eighty years old. They say he got his name because he'd survive us all, survive off our rotting flesh if he had too. He made up for Thorn's lack of tattoos by having one on every inch except his face. I had no idea why. His hideous face was the one thing he should've covered. A complete asshole as far as I could tell, he was happily married to a plump woman named Ida and had seven grandkids.

My brother Dimple occupied the crowd, singing "Witchy Woman", but of course exactly like Elvis would sing it. A client turned member, Dimple owed Kingpin a large debt for services rendered. No one would tell me why Dimple hired the Royal Bastards to begin with. What happened at Royal Road stayed there. My brothers were sworn to secrecy, they'd say, but there was actually an NDA to back up their words.

Sadist guarded the door. Out of all my brothers here, I knew him the least. Actually, I was surprised he was here with the Halloween Party going on. Like many of my brothers he worked at Royal Road. We all did at times, but

Sadist managed the basement where the freaky sexual shit happened.

Riff blew smoke in Eve's face, and I'd liked to have slapped him. They didn't give two shits about finding Wolf's killer. They'd said as much when I first talked to them when they got to Bootsies. Kingpin warned them to keep their noses clean, meaning don't shoot up the place or kill anyone.

"How does he expect us to fuck with our peckers tied behind our backs?" Buzzard complained.

"Wolf just started prospecting. He doesn't even wear his cut." Riff didn't like that Grady led a double life as he put it. Kingpin casted a wide net, wanting members who had lived outside of the club. The Nashville Chapter of the Royal Bastards MC had grown like a wildfire much like the city. Riff, on the other hand, wanted all our members to work and live at Royal Road. "Wolf was about to be another part-timer."

My brothers were bored, I could tell. They were getting ready to leave. If they didn't take Eve with them, I could convince her to leave Tennessee. Go back to Arkansas. Then Riff pulled out Grady's phone and his text to Eve. Fucking, Wolf. The thought that she had something going on with that old man tore me up. Instantly, I knew I couldn't let her leave. If she went back to Arkansas alone, she'd be in danger. I could take her, but it'd risk both of us. But that wasn't why I couldn't let her go. I wanted her to

stay. I wanted her. An animal deep inside me growled thinking of her with Wolf or another man, for that matter. And I couldn't quit thinking about her and Wolf together. Had she been fooling me?

Jealousy flooded my emotions. "Show me your phone," I demanded when my brothers left.

Seeing that Eve read Grady's texts and sent an eggplant emoji back shocked me. I didn't take Eve for a liar. A fucking eggplant. She denied it. I thought of my dick in Eve's hand just moments before we found the dead body. I wanted to shove my dick in her mouth and shut her up. Nevertheless, I didn't have time to think of who else could've messed with Eve's phone and why. The lights went out. Eve squeezed my hand. Of course she did, Wolf was dead. His eggplant cold, too. As much as my possessiveness clouded my thoughts, I knew nothing good happened in the dark. Once the room lit up, I headed straight for the front. There I found a crowd around Sadist's body. An ice pick protruded from his neck. Who had an ice pick? The bartender. I'd already come to the conclusion Jasper killed Wolf. Earlier, Ford had relayed the story about Eve almost being abducted the night before, saying Grady almost caught the guy in the ski mask who ran off. He ran over his foot. Jasper stupidly limped to work. The man was a few cards shy of a deck and that was the only reason I hadn't nabbed him already. He'd been working for someone else. Celie maybe. Pleasantly distracted by Eve, I'd not figured it out. At first, I didn't care to. That was until Eve was involved.

Riff told us to pick our suspect so I grabbed Jasper, not thinking anyone would grab Eve. She struck Buzzard in the balls, and I took my chance to secure her. Gagging her, I placed the tiger mask over her head so she couldn't see where I was taking her. After all, Buzzard was right. Those were our rules. No uninvited guests. I couldn't take a prisoner to Royal Road casually riding bitch.

I had to take Eve to Kingpin myself. I'd given anything for her safety. And I didn't have myself to give anymore. I belonged to the Royal Bastards MC and Kingpin already. And I didn't regret that choice. Being an outlaw gave me a freedom I never had before. Unfortunately, there was only one thing that could save Eve besides getting her out of the state. And even then, back in Arkansas she might not be safe. My brothers knew of her now and as long as the Asphalt Gods were our enemy, she'd be in peril. Well, it wasn't unfortunate for me. Only one thing could save her. She'd have to become one of us.

Unlike the Asphalt Gods, we didn't patch women. Eve would become mine, my property. It'd taken years for me to get used to the biker lifestyle, so I was sure Eve wouldn't take kindly to getting a tattoo saying she was mine or any of the other gestures we'd have to make to pull this off. As I held her on the front of my bike, I longed to really have her. As it was, we would have to pretend. I wouldn't be pretending. I could only hope Eve liked me enough. She sure seemed to in the breakroom. I liked my lips tasting her

there. Speeding down the road, I tried to wipe her text with Wolf out of my mind.

Royal Road was known for its Halloween parties. Hell, Royal Road was the best place to party, no matter the occasion. Last week, we had a wild as all get out baby shower for Horror's ol' lady that turned into a baby shower for several pregnant women she knew. Opry hired some male strippers just for that night. So, I was not surprised by the scene when I stepped into the clubhouse. Actually, I'd become numb to it. When I was there, I was usually tasked with security anyhow, and though I'd look like I was there to party, I watched the tables, the gamblers, the men watching the strippers. Opry ran Royal Road in a management capacity, taking care of all the entertainment. When I stepped in with Eve, he thought I'd brought a girl for him to audition. A lot of the strippers were just auditioning. They didn't come in without being blindfolded somehow or another. There was a steady stream of women wanting a place at Royal Road. They'd get to keep their tips, but they weren't on the payroll.

Taking Eve in front of Kingpin had been worse than I imagined. Kingpin in his large, elaborately carved wooden throne with the red velvet enjoyed toying with us. Riff had already told him everything, even that Eve was a virgin. I tried to leave without becoming part of his show, but Junebug, one of Kingpin's whores, drew her gun. Even though I tried to play it cool, when I stepped out of my boots and slipped down my pants, my limp dick gave me away. I took no pleasure in taking a woman against her will. Especially not innocent Eve. I'd been so close to taking her virginity on my own. To be coerced to force her turned my stomach.

Memphis sank to her knees and fluffed me in no time. Being one of our sweetbutts, our club whore, she knew exactly how to get me hard. Hell, Junebug knew too. They'd warmed my bed a time or two, the both of them together, when I first got here. That was before I learned exactly how much they got around. Kingpin might as well be a pimp with how the girls were pretty much up for sale to anyone privileged enough to play here. After a STD test I thankfully passed, I hadn't fooled with any of the club whores again. I'd gone from the whores to the hang arounds, the girls who rode bikes, the biker bitches. If I thought of Steph, I'd lose my woody. Kingpin wanted a show. He wanted to see blood. Taking Eve to the middle of the orgy, I made sure to put something between us and the nasty carpet. I tried my best to make her bleed with my hand. I thought that once I did, I could cover her and pound the floor beneath her ass to fool Kingpin into thinking he won. After all, this was a game to him. He'd caught me lying, and he wanted to punish me.

I pulled up my mask to look and saw the red blood on my fingers, but I also saw Kingpin's black polished toes. There was no getting out of here without fucking Eve's brains out, as he put it. Shifting gears, I thought of how bad I wanted her earlier while I tasted her pussy. Licking my lips,

I still tasted her salty essence. Eve was mine for the taking now. It was so wrong. Eve was gagged and bound and helpless beneath me. Something about it though, knowing I had no choice, turned me on. Lining my dick up with her bloody cunt, I jutted my hips to shove inside her tight snatch. It felt better than I could've dreamed. I'd never taken anyone's virginity before.

Leaning on my elbows, I took her shoulders into my hands to hold her as my dick broke completely inside of her warm snatch. God damn. Eve felt amazing. I'd gone where no man had gone before. Sliding back, I plowed again and again. Her pussy a vice squeezing my dick egged me on until I felt I might break her in two if I didn't ease up. Her body trembled under me, and I remembered she couldn't scream if she needed to. However, that fact never stopped me. I enjoyed it. Her helpless. Eve was mine. Her pussy all mine. I'd tattoo her with my property patch and dare anyone to even look at her. Her heart would be mine as well, in time. After our show here, I planned to take her up to my bedroom and do this again but with our masks off. As of now, I pounded her pussy wanting nothing but to get off so Kingpin would let us be. I longed to take her upstairs and taste her lips, to hear her cries of pleasure, her cries of pain. I wanted to take my time, find out what she liked. She'd never done anything with any man, and I wanted to be her man. The only one. The thought of that and exploring every inch of her had me coming in no time.

Drawing my cock out of her, I spilled my seed on her stomach so Kingpin could see we were finished here. Satisfied he walked off. Immediately, I took off my mask, a fucking unicorn and Eve's tiger mask. I took down the gag, expecting her to cry. Searching her eyes, I asked if she was okay. Eve's hooded eyes let me know she'd really enjoyed what just happened. I roared internally. Picking her up, I rushed her through the front of the club wanting to get her in my bed. I'd convince her to truly be mine. Not just to keep the Royal Bastards MC from killing her. After a night in my bed, she'd be begging for that tattoo, my property patch. Passing the buffet, I asked if she was hungry. In any case, I planned to fuck her again, and she'd need all her strength. No. Eve had been a virgin. My mind racing, I thought of how she deserved a night of more than fucking. I planned to make love to her until dawn and pick it back up tomorrow and fuck her.

That's when she told me about Ford.

Fuck, I'd fucked up. Eve was right. I knew Jasper had been working for someone, but I hadn't known who. Our night of love making would have to wait. My brothers Riff and Dimple had Ford with them taking Sadist out to Franklin, to Delbert's pig farm. Kingpin had a deal with Delbert. Delbert wasn't even the man's name. That had been the name of the farm. We paid the mysterious old man who called himself Delbert to dispose of bodies there. Paid him in drugs mostly, and he kept his mouth shut.

While Eve showered, I called my brothers with no luck. Fuck, I didn't even know if there'd be a signal out on the farm in Franklin. My cellphone was in my pants in Kingpin's throne room, so I couldn't look up the number to Bootsies to ask what happened to Thorn or Buzzard who'd been going after Eve's goth friend Donette. I had a dozen brothers downstairs that I could count on, but none that I wanted to know about Eve. The less my brothers knew about Eve the better. I didn't need word getting back to Leviathan she was Fighting Cocks daughter before I could get a proper tattoo on her.

Walking in on Eve crying in the bathroom, broke my heart. I'd done a billion dreadful things since leaving Columbus but having sex with Eve like that had been the worst. Instead of comforting her, I punched the wall. It didn't matter what she wanted. Once she had a property patch, she'd be safe. That mark would mean she made the choice between her father's club and ours. It would mean she was mine and my brothers couldn't touch her. For now, we had to get to Riff and Dimple. I'd not killed someone for the club before. Ford was about to be my first. I didn't know why he tried to take Eve last night, but I planned to find out. It couldn't have been good. Then he killed Wolf, maybe Sadist, too.

In this situation, Eve had to come with me. I strapped a gun on her and snuck her out the front door. This time we would be on my hog. When I bought it, my brothers in Charleston said my Harley-Davidson, Street Glide Special looked like a police Harley with the batwing fairing and LED headlamp. Little did they know, I almost got it in the two-tone blue and white one. Old habits die hard and all. Thankfully, I picked the metallic grey and black finish. The Nashville boys hadn't said anything, yet.

Fuck, the rain started.

"If you weren't already mine, I'd have to hood you," I said as we came to the gate. As we approached my brother Cricket, our guard, I explained to Eve, "No one comes to Royal Road unannounced. If I didn't hood you before, I'd be chained up in the basement right now. You, too. I'm going to tell my buddy Cricket you're my girl, and you're not going to argue."

"But we're leaving."

"Coming or going, doesn't matter."

Eve didn't say a word as I explained to Cricket, she was fixing to be my woman.

"Didn't you just bring in a prisoner? Kingpin aware of this?" Cricket had to be sure. His ass was on the line too. He'd write it down, take a mental picture or a real one. I had no idea how he and Gunn remembered everyone who came through the gate, but they were thorough.

Thankfully, there wasn't much more than a drizzle on the way to Franklin. When I stopped at the back entrance of the farm to give a signal for Delbert to let me in, I found

the gate left open. Speeding through the opening and down the bumpy dirt road, I hoped Eve was holding on. Reaching the barn, I spotted Dimple's 1955 Pink Cadillac Fleetwood. Yes, one just like the King drove. The top was down. I parked beside it and saw Riff passed out inside. I placed my fingers on his neck before I decided if he was dead or not. He'd live, but he was out cold. Delbert stepped out of the dark with a rifle.

Recognizing my cut, he put the barrel down. "You just missed the action." He explained, "Dimple is up at the house having some supper. Riff will be okay. Those boys they had with them was dragging the body out to the slaughterhouse and got the better of me." He rubbed the back of his neck. "Looks like they got to Riff too. Dimple had already started heading to the house to fetch a ham I said he could have. Those boys ran off with ol' Bessy."

"Bessy?"

"Yeah. Y'all owe me a truck."

Understanding Ford and Louis stole Delbert's pickup truck, I figured they'd head back to Nashville.

"Do you know where Ford lives?" I asked Eve.

"Downtown somewhere. Donette knows. And I know where she lives, and I have a key. Well, I did. It's in my purse at Bootsies."

"Let's go and get it."

"Probably locked up for the night."

With a few murders reported, I doubted it. We made our way back into downtown Nashville. When we made it to Bootsies, I looked at my watch, and it was nearing five am. Being fall, it was still dark as night. I'd been right about the honky-tonk. Three squad cars lined the front of the building. Of course, Eve and I decided to go into the back.

We creeped around to the alley on my motorcycle. "Go straight to the breakroom, get your purse and come straight out."

Eve disappeared through the back door. Shutting off the engine, I waited for her to return. We'd go to her friends and get a lead on Ford. I'd leave Eve at her friend's house and go after Ford myself. Everything was going to work out. I was pleased with this plan. But Eve didn't return. Not after five minutes. Not after ten. I couldn't wait any longer to go find her. Stepping into the back of Bootsies, I was careful, even though the back hallway had been dark. Coming out the small door between the bathrooms, I ran right into Celie.

"What are you doing back here?" She crossed her arms. "Cops are on it now."

"Have you seen Eve?"

"Yeah, she just left with Ford."

"What? When? Where?"

"Yes, they just left out the front door, like we're supposed to. How'd you get in the back."

I grabbed her and tried not to shake her. "Celie, Ford killed Grady."

The woman about fell on the floor. I caught her by the elbow.

"Where did he say she was taking her?"

"Eve made it a point to tell me she was going home if I needed her. Maybe he's taking her home?"

"Where's that?"

Celie gave me an address, nearby and downtown, and I luckily made it out the back door without any of the officers seeing me. Getting to the address, I made it up the stairs before I realized Eve had already told me she lived in Cottontown. Wondering who's address Celie gave me, I knocked on the door anyhow. There wasn't an answer. Why would there be? It was five in the fucking morning. I started to leave but heard a scream. Just like I was trained, I kicked in the door. Rushing to the cries, I turned on the light to find a couple in bed. Thorn, his muscular black back with the Royal Bastard's patch covered Donette's milky skin. This was Eve's friend's place. Obviously, they'd been fucking, but Thorn lifted all the way up so I could see his big cock was still inside her.

"Holy shit," I complained.

"Hey, man. What gives?"

I turned away from the show. "Ford's our killer, and he's got Eve. Celie gave me this address."

"Ford?" Thorn asked.

"The bartender? The one I was after?"

"No, the other one."

Thorn clearly wasn't invested in this. I told him, "Eve's with me now, my girl, and Ford's our murderer."

"Alright then. Let's go."

"Eve pays rent here but hasn't moved in yet. She lives out in Cottontown," Donette explained. She'd moved away from Thorn and covered herself with a sheet.

"Do you think Ford would take her there?"

"I don't know why he would. Her Gran's there, and she'll shoot him if he tries anything. She about shot me last time I visited. I'll show you the way."

Thorn and Donette threw on their clothes. We were all out the door in no time, heading forty minutes north to Cottontown. I followed Thorn who took his directions from Donette who rode bitch on his bike. When we pulled into

the driveway, Jasper was backing out in a yellow Subaru Baja.

"I'm after him." Thorn left Donette with me, telling her, "Stay put."

Shutting off my hog, I put my finger to my lips to let Donette know I'd be sneaking up to the house. Leaving her, I creeped up the long gravel driveway to see a motorcycle parked in front of the porch. It was an older model Harley, a fatboy, worn and dirty.

"What the hell?"

The lights were on inside, and I could see through the screen door a big man and Eve screaming at one another. I rushed the door and was inside, my gun drawn on him in no time. Before me, stood Eve and what had to be her father. The old man was grey and plump but held her eyes and features. No cut, he wore a blue and white flannel and Wrangler jeans. His hands were in his pockets. Eve had the gun I gave her in her hands, pointed at him already. Tears streaked her face.

"What's going on?" I asked, my eyes on her gun.

"My dad killed Grady. Killed Wolf."

My confusion showed on my face.

Eve expounded, "He's the one who hired Ford to snatch me and deliver me to him. I'm sure Ford killed Grady, but it was all my dad's fault."

"Where's Ford?"

Eve's dad spoke up. "He left out before my daughter got to her gun."

Our heads whipped around as we heard the gunshot out front. All together we ran out of the house heading to the end of the drive. We heard two more shots before we reached Donette on the ground. Ford laid beside her a gun in his hand. She'd been shot in the shoulder. Screaming out bloody murder, Donette was very much alive. Thorn stood over Ford. He'd not missed. Ford was dead, shot square in the chest. Thorn's gun was trained on Eve's dad now. The man put up his hands but just a hair. Eve dropped her pistol and sank to Donette. Taking off my jacket, she used it to apply pressure to her friend's shoulder. With my gun pointed at Fighting Cock as well, I waited for Eve to react. She gazed up at her dad.

"I'm not going back with you," she screamed at her father.

"Eve Angel. It's not safe for you here. You wouldn't understand." The man slurred his words.

Eve cried, speaking between sobs, "I've found out it's not safe... You almost killed my best friend, dad... You did kill my friends... I'm staying here with Donette."

"These Royal Bastards will skin you alive because of me."

"Damn straight. We're going to kill you, Fighting Cock," Thorn told him.

The man's eyes got wide as he realized that we already knew his identity. He was three sheets to the wind. Eve hadn't been kidding about him being a drunk.

"No. They won't. I'm one of them now dad, you don't have to worry about me," Eve said to him, shocking the hell out of me.

"What do you mean?"

"I belong to Hallow. Their president Kingpin approves. I've gotten a property patch and everything, so I can't go back to Arkansas with you now."

"Eve, how could you?" Her father braced himself, his hands on his knees.

"I guess you should've told me about the danger I was in before I came to Tennessee."

"But you ran off. You won't take my calls."

Eve protruded her chin, pouting.

"You're just like your mother. I couldn't keep her safe, and I'll be damned if I let anyone kill you."

Eve wouldn't look at him. I felt somewhat bad for the man, but she'd been the one that knew him, she lived with him. I'm sure she had plenty of reasons for wanting to get away from him.

I assured him, "Eve's safe with me."

"And once you're done with her, you're a Royal Bastard and she's still my daughter. What then?"

"I'm not going to be done with her."

"We'll see. I'll be back with fifty men."

Thorn rushed to Fighting Cock and had his gun to the old man's temple.

"Hallow." Eve's eyes pleaded with me. "I want him to go back to Arkansas in one piece. Please don't kill him."

Thorn spoke to me. "Sounds like you two had a busy night. You know we should take him in, Hallow. Kingpin hears we didn't, and we'll be pig shit."

"It'll all be on me. You weren't even here," I said to Thorn.

"Do what you want. Your girl, your call."

"Go back to Arkansas now, leave Eve be and you'll escape with your life," I said to Eve's dad, cocking my gun. "Otherwise, Kingpin knows where your daughter and mother are."

Thorn let him go and backed away, his gun still on him. I waited for him to go but the man didn't budge.

"My mother's back in Arkansas." Fighting Cock garbled out.

"What are you talking about dad?"

"Your brother picked your Gran up this afternoon, right after you left for work. I suspect they're back home by now."

The fucker just told us his son had been here too. That he had a son. I gave Thorn a sideways glance.

Eve asked him, "What did you plan to do with me?"

He kicked the gravel. "Ford feller was supposed to deliver you to me this morning at the border, so you wouldn't be no trouble when we got your Gran. So, you'd come home, finally. When he didn't, I came to get you myself."

"You pay him?"

"Yeah, in cash. Check his pockets. You can keep it. Think of it as an engagement present." The man looked me in the eyes. "I expect you to make her an honest woman."

"Dad," Eve complained.

"I will," I promised him.

Thorn reached down and pulled an envelope out of Ford's jacket and handed it to me. I tucked it inside of my cut.

Her father complained.

"I'll give it to her once it's safe," I reassured him. With a dead body on her lawn the last thing Eve needed was a bloody envelope full of cash.

Thorn and I kept our guns drawn, but we let them say their goodbyes.

"Where's Gran?" Eve asked her dad.

"She's going to the old folks home back home. I've sold her house and furniture to pay for it. Everything's out except your belongings. Buyers will be here next week. You'll have to give them the keys. I suspect you have somewhere to go."

"I have an apartment," Eve said. "Now get, before they change their minds."

Her father hung his head and turned to walk away. Thorn and I kept our guns up until he raced away on his motorcycle. We had a mess to clean up again, two dead bodies because Thorn had killed Jasper right before Ford shot Donette. And since Ford had killed Grady, we couldn't just take him to Delbert's farm. The police were already at Bootsies investigating Grady's murder. Eve agreed to use Ford's truck to drive Donette to the hospital to get the bullet out of her shoulder. Ford had exchanged Delbert's ride for his own once in Nashville. We'd have to retrieve the farmer's truck, too.

Thorn and I dragged Jasper's lifeless body from the cab to situate him beside Ford on the driveway. Thorn then helped Donette into the passenger side of the truck as I went to Eve on the driver's side. Her window rolled down.

"Am I missing anything? I don't have to worry about someone else taking you from me."

"I don't think so," Eve replied, drying her eyes.

Thorn added, "Jasper killed Sadist. He confessed before he tried to knife me."

I handed Eve Thorn's gun and took mine back. "You shot them when Ford shot Donette. We were never here."

"Right." Eve nodded her head. I was glad she didn't argue. "My dad was never here either. Oh, what about big Earl. I guess Ford killed him, too?"

"We'll let the cops figure it out." I instructed Eve to call the police once she got to the nearest hospital in Gallatin. She had her cell phone now. She told me how Ford nabbed her right after she got it from the breakroom. We exchanged numbers.

Thorn and I did our best to erase any trace of us or Fighting Cock being at Eve's house before we left. Eve would have to talk to the police. They'd be out here for the bodies, so I couldn't stick around or pick her up from the hospital like I wanted to. The ride back to Nashville was excruciating. I worried for Eve, afraid her father would turn around and come back to get her. Or that somehow, Kingpin had been watching me and planned to have our boys snatch her.

Walking into the throne room for my phone, erased my fears. Everyone had left, except my President curled up on the floor asleep with Memphis and Junebug at his sides. I'd have to tell him what happened tomorrow. I retrieved my clothes, belt, boots and Eve's shoes. I checked to make sure my wallet and phone were in my jeans. They were. Up in my room, Thorn snored as I put Eve's number in my phone. I sent her a text. "What's up?" I fell asleep waiting for a reply.

A chime on my phone woke me. It was two p.m. Eve had sent a text back finally. It simply read, "Donette's dead."

"Fuck."

Thorn's bed was made. I called him and relayed the news. "Fuck, man."

"I'm going to the hospital. You coming?"

"No. I just met that girl. I never planned to have anything else to do with the chic. Sorry, man. Give my condolences to your girl though."

I understood, but I didn't feel the same way about Eve. My heart ached for her. I couldn't mount my Harley fast enough.

CHAPTER 9

EVE

Hallow walked into the waiting room, and I'd never been so happy to see anyone in my life. I'd slept in an uncomfortable chair on and off, when I wasn't crying with Donette's family who had gathered in the waiting room with me. After I called the police and relayed the news about Ford and Jasper, I called Donette's mom and woke her. My best friend had to have surgery, and I wasn't authorized to make those types of decisions. It being an emergency, the surgery was on way before Donette's family got here. We never expected her not to make it through. The cops were here questioning me just as the doctor came out and told us Donette had died. He said she expired or something, and I lost it. The officers told me to come into Nashville Monday to give my statement. They took the keys to Ford's truck. Although Donette had died, she was in a room where the family could be with her before the funeral home picked her up. Exhaustion was my only comfort, numbing the pain of losing a true friend. However, guilt festered adding to my sorrow.

But now, Hallow hugged me to him. The smell of leather flooded my senses as I wrapped my arms under his motorcycle vest. He was warm and alive. I wanted to get out of here. I hadn't gone in to say goodbye to Donette. I couldn't. Not even saying goodbye to her family, I tugged Hallow out of the hospital. He straddled his motorcycle, and I was about to climb on.

"Where to?" he asked.

I thought about going home and crashing in my bed at Gran's before I remembered the scene there. Mine and Donette's apartment was out of the question too.

"I don't know. Anywhere but here."

"My place?"

I shook my head. I certainly didn't want to go to Royal Road.

"I know somewhere," Hallow said, offering his hand.

Climbing behind him, I pressed my face into his leather and draped my arms around his middle locking my hands together. The roar and the wind took me away. Lost on the drive, I didn't care where we went as long as Hallow was with me.

We rode for about an hour before we crossed a wooden bridge and went up a steep driveway to a small cabin in the woods.

"I'll have to be in Nashville tomorrow."

"We're in Scottsboro, near Back Creek," Hallow explained.

I didn't know where that was and said as much.

"We're still in Nashville, only in the forest. Only about fifteen minutes away from Broadway." Hallow unlocked the door, clarifying, "I was looking at this place. Told you my room at Royal Road was temporary. I still had the key."

"What about the owners?" I asked, stepping inside.

"Kingpin owns it, and I haven't told him if I want the place, yet. It's furnished, but no one lives here. No one will be out here. It's just us."

Just us, those words comforted me. Hallow stepped in close, sheltering me in his large arms again. My hands ran up his vest, up his muscular back. I rested my head on his chest. His hand cupped my head. "Want to get some rest?"

"Yes," I breathed against his t-shirt, but I didn't want to move.

Hallow scooped me up and carried me to the bedroom, laying me on the bed. He joined me, flopping down beside me. I crashed into his side, laying my head in the crook of his arm. That arm tugged me close. I closed my eyes and cried myself to sleep.

When I woke, my head laid on a pillow. Hallow was gone. I felt cold. Pulling the covers up and over me, I shivered. A single bedside lamp lit the room. Sitting up, I saw it was also dark outside. How long had I slept? I heard a door creak open. Hallow stepped into the room in nothing but a towel wrapped around his waist. His hair wet, he'd been in the shower. He looked as delicious as always, but his concerned expression warmed my heart.

Smiling, he regarded me. "You're up. You hungry?"

With a pout, I swayed my head. I couldn't eat. Feeling a bit sick to my stomach, I was still in shock from everything that had happened. Hallow sat on the side of the bed noticing I had the covers over me.

"You cold? I can crawl back in bed with you," he joked.

"Please," I choked out.

Hallow wasted no time removing his towel and getting under the covers with me. I caught a glimpse of his erect dick as he did and shivered in anticipation. His hot naked body zipped against mine as he clutched the back of my head and went straight for my lips. I returned his kiss with a fervor savoring the taste of him. I needed a drink. Hallow, he was the good stuff. The best shot of whiskey I could ask for. He wrenched my shirt over my head, flinging it away. I hadn't had on a bra since our romp in the breakroom. His hands cupped my breasts instantly as our

mouths joined again. While we necked, Hallow undid my jeans and pushed them down past my bottom. I wiggled and shoved them down the rest of the way with my feet until they were gone. Our naked bodies surged together while our kiss grew softer. Running my hands down, I tried to touch every inch of him at once. His chest, his strong back, his butt, his abs. My tongue twisted with his as I felt his tight hairy abs against my fingers. I went lower to seize his stiff erection. Sliding my hand up and down the length of it, I clutched his balls. Then I ran my thumb over the spongy head, feeling the moisture there.

Reacting, Hallow grunted into my mouth and began to get up. My arms rushed around his back as he flipped us until I was on top of him. His lips left mine as he pressed me up to sit and straddle him. His brown eyes were all over my breasts before his hands caught them. Coming up, he captured my nipple in his mouth. Meanwhile, his dick slipped between my legs rubbing my clit just right. Wow. Moaning, I enjoyed the amazing sensation. His rough beard rubbing against my skin and soft mouth exploring my delicate flesh made me feral. Thrusting my hips, I rubbed my wet pussy on his hard length as he sucked and bit the flesh of my chest. As Hallow nibbled up to my neck, his hand reached down to line his cock up with my entrance. I sat down, helping him along as his dick inched inside of me.

Oh, how I needed this. Hallow filled me up and made me feel whole.

He flipped us again, and I was on my back learning he hadn't been inside me much at all. His dick surged now, skewering me. Just like before it hurt, though not nearly as much. He steered my knees up and apart to really drive deep and proved me wrong. I cried out before his dick pushed all the right buttons. My back arched. My toes curled. Hallow smirked and only drove harder, making me scream. Unlike before when we were forced to, I could see his face hanging over me. His features dripped with a ravenous hunger as he moved inside me. I felt how he looked, completely starved.

Licking his lips, he watched my reactions to his lurches. He watched as my cries turned to whimpers begging him to go on. Hallow built a fire in my belly. I was getting close to burning to a crisp. Our sweaty foreheads met before our lips collided. As Hallow kissed me, soft and deep, his thrusts followed suit. Soft and deep. Somehow that only made matters worse. My blaze grew uncontrollable. Hallow, rolling his hips, tossed gasoline on it. Watching him melt in the flames, I felt him burst inside me. He hadn't pulled out in time. He crashed beside me on the bed.

Thinking maybe I could go to the bathroom and get his cum out of me, I started to get up. Hallow heaved me on top of him and held me down. "You're not going anywhere."

"I'm not on the pill. You're going to get me pregnant."

Hallow reached down and cupped my pussy as to hold his cum in. "So? You're mine. Have my baby."

He had to be joking. I snorted.

"Marry me?"

Huffing, I rolled my eyes.

"Eve, I'm serious. Move in here with me."

"Maybe," I answered him. I started to think about what I'd have to do about Gran's house and Donette's apartment. Nevertheless, I didn't want to think of anything but Hallow. I wiped my mind clean of anything but him.

"Maybe?" Hallow sat up, pulling me with him. His dick was already hard again. "Maybe you'll suck my cock a while."

I smirked. "Maybe."

After I said it, Hallow shoved me down, and I obliged, taking his big dick into my mouth. Though inexperienced, I did my best and felt quite sexy while he watched me. He groaned his approval while he stroked my hair. I felt like a goddess pleasuring him. Soon Hallow hauled me up to straddle him. "Remember that bull. You're going to ride me like Taco."

This time with Hallow's mess inside me, it was much easier to impel myself on his hard dick. Like on the mechanical bull, I wobbled and lurched as Hallow held my hips, thrashing under me. Our eyes locked as he came in me again almost instantly. I tried to get off him, but he seized my hips. Held me on top of him, his cock in me. His eyes danced like it was funny.

"Lordalmighty. You really might get me pregnant. Don't you own any condoms?"

"Not for you. You're mine, aren't you?"

I didn't know about all that, even if I had told my dad and he'd told Kingpin as much. My chin shook back and forth.

"I'm the only man who's come in your pussy, and I'm going to be the only man going forward to ever. You hear?"

"Whatever," I said.

"Whatever," Hallow exclaimed, moving out from under me. He disappeared to the bathroom, and I could hear the toilet flush. I followed him. I had to go pee, too. I passed him while he was going out and shut the door and locked it. I took a minute and wiped good and deep, but I knew Hallow had come deep inside me. Nonetheless, I didn't want to think of anything. I wouldn't worry about it. Hallow wiggled the door handle and knocked. After I washed my hands, I let him in.

Hallow stood before me naked, and I couldn't get enough of him.

"Lock me out. Just for that, turn around."

"No. You going to spank me or something?"

"No." Hallow chuckled, stroking his erection again.

I turned around, leaning my hands on the sink expecting to be filled up again. Hallow, standing up behind me, steered my hips back, preparing me. I longed for the sensation of this man's dick inside me. But he hauled off and struck my ass. Hard.

Lordalmighty. I hollered out, "You said you wouldn't."

Without a word, Hallow wrapped my long hair around his fist and pulled it, pulling my head back. He slapped my ass again. This time it stung, but I didn't complain. I bayed as he rubbed it where it'd hurt. Moisture seeped between my pussy's lips as he'd started the unbearable itch again. Hallow's hand ran down to feel the fluid. He petted my wet pussy, and I thought he was going to fuck me again. But Hallow surprised me. Letting go of my hair, he opened the medicine cabinet in front of me, took something and shut it. Unexpectedly, Hallow drew my arms back, my wrists together, wrapping medical tape around them to secure them.

"Hey," I complained.

He bit off the extra length. "Be quiet, Eve."

"Make me," I said, as I struggled to get out of the tape.

Hallow pressed me against the sink and took the tape and wrapped it around my head, around my mouth, like a gag.

When my hands were bound behind me and my mouth was muzzled, he struck my ass again. I whimpered into the tape around my mouth. Hallow shushed me, and said, "I want to fuck you like this again, on my own terms."

Then he slipped his dick inside me from behind, giving me what I craved. This was a brand-new sensation as he tickled a new place inside me. I wouldn't fight. My body trembled as he worked me up anew. His hand ran down my stomach to rub my clit as he made long strokes in and out of me. In the mirror in front of us, I watched my own face gagged with the tape, contort as he clasped my breasts and fucked me hard again. His other hand seized my hair again and held my head back the whole time. My arms and head restrained, I was completely at his mercy, just like during the orgy, and I freaking loved every moment of it. Just when I thought it couldn't get better, Hallow bit at my neck as he rocked his hips. My body convulsed. Once I had my moment, I observed him beaming in the mirror, pleased with himself as I quaked. But he wasn't done. He held my hips, still plunging in and out of me.

It was a longtime until Hallow came again.

He was the energizer bunny, and I was almost out of juice. We changed positions many times. My hands still bound behind me, he sat me on the sink, my legs spread wide as he charged inside me. Looking down we watched his long dick slip in and out of my entrance. My mouth occupied, Hallow laid kisses on my breasts and neck. He licked the side of my face and ears as he fucked me. Then he sat on the toilet's lid and towed me on top of his cock, my back to his chest, my legs together. He bounced me like a doll on his rod. We ended up in the jacuzzi tub, running a bubble bath in almost that same position, though my legs splayed his thighs. I didn't mind it. I'd never had sex before Hallow and now I'd be satisfied if Hallow's dick never left my pussy. The fact that he kept me gagged and tied up didn't faze me, either. I was turned on that he was so turned on.

In the water, our wet bodies skidded against each other, adding a different friction. The warm water covering my sexy bits felt amazing with Hallow deep inside me. He kissed the back of my shoulder as I rocked up and down on his length. He turned off the water and carefully washed my back. All while his dick throbbed inside me.

"Turn around," he demanded.

Awkwardly, with my hands tied, I stood and turned and sank to my knees. Hallow held his dick wanting me to sit on it again. It was easier now but different in the water. He directed my legs to go around his waist. Once more, I was confronted with a new sensation. Hallow had to hold my back as he leaned me and lovingly washed my torso, each breast and my stomach. Faced with him, I wanted to follow suit, but my hands were bound. He soaped up his hard pecs, his strong shoulders and thick neck. As he washed his arms, I studied his tattoos. Skulls, roses, crowns, daggers, I would ask what they all meant another time since I couldn't now. All lathered, Hallow stirred more purposefully under me. We slid against each other effortlessly now. He was about to blow his load again. His desperate jerky movements sent me to the edge as well. Hallow came inside me as I got off at the same time.

Finally, he heaved down the tape.

"I can't go again. I'm tired. I'm starved," I panted.

Hallow agreed, "Once we're clean, I'll order some food. What do you want?"

"Anything." At least I was hungry now. Hallow released my hands. We washed up quickly.

Stepping out of the bath, I let Hallow wrap me in a towel. I didn't want to put his ex's clothes back on, so I didn't. The biker ordered Chinese, and I ate General Taos in bed in nothing but his big black t-shirt. He put on his jeans, thankfully. If he pulled out his dick again, I might not ever get to leave. Speaking of which, I told him, I'd have to go to the police station tomorrow morning and go home to Gran's. "I need to get my stuff out and move it to my

apartment. No telling when the new owners want to move in. I need to call Celie about what's going on at Bootsies. I missed work today."

"I'm sure they didn't open. I'll make sure you get to the police station and home, but you need some time off to rest, to mourn."

Agreeing with Hallow, I let him hold me all night. We slept like two people that had been fucking for hours upon hours.

CHAPTER 10

EVE

I woke early while Hallow still slept. In the morning light with my shock from all the death fading, everything felt different. Immediately, not comfortable, I hugged myself. Glancing around the strange cabin and at the biker, I wondered what I'd done. Examining the marks on my wrists, I felt dirty. Probably knocked up for all I knew, my choices felt like they were no longer my own. Overwhelming grief forced my hand into spending the better part of the night having wild, unprotected sex with a man I barely knew, a biker at that. I told my dad I belonged to this man. Searching for my phone, I had to get ahold of Donette's family about her arrangements. I didn't want to miss her funeral. I hadn't even gone in to say goodbye to her at the hospital. But I couldn't think of my best friend dead. Grady and Earl dying was bad enough. Grady had kids, and Earl, well, I didn't know much about him. But they'd lived their lives. Donette was so young. Not that she didn't live her life. She sure did, but still she was taken too soon. Ford and Jasper were a shock, as well. In the course of an evening, five people I called friends had died.

When I thought about how my father caused all this, all because of me, I didn't know if I could ever show my face around Bootsies or to Donette's family again. Then I wondered if dad got back to Arkansas okay. He was a drunk and no good, but it didn't mean I didn't worry for him. I hadn't even gotten to say goodbye to my Gran. My phone was almost out of charge, and my charger was at home. Well, there was one in my car too. But my car was still in the parking garage on Church Street. It'd been there all weekend, and I'd be lucky if the city hadn't towed it.

I decided to dial my brother, Hob. It went straight to his voicemail. Eight a.m. on a Monday, he was likely in class since he had college to attend. I left him a message. Reluctantly, I called my dad next. Voicemail again. Dern.

Hob texted me saying he was in class.

"Sorry. Did dad get back?"

"Said he wasn't coming back without you."

"I sent him back, alone. He's not back?"

"No."

"Thanks for warning me he was coming, by the way."

"I've got class."

"Where's Gran?"

Hob never texted back. I searched the web for Senior living facilities back home in Flipping, Arkansas. There was only the one, Shady Pines. Surely dad wouldn't have put her farther away. I called them asking after Frannie Newberry. They transferred me to her room.

"Eve. Whore. They done kidnapped me."

"I heard."

"They say I need to be in this old folk's home, but you can tell them I'm fine. I know I can't control myself sometimes, but I'm fine."

"Yes, Gr... Fran. You are. You are fine." Really my Gran had nothing wrong with her but the Tourette's.

"This place is Hell."

I felt horrible that I couldn't go to Arkansas and break her out, but I also knew dad had moved her because she was in danger in Tennessee.

"They don't even have cable television. Only Netflix. How can I watch the news and weather?"

"I'm sorry, Fran."

"You'll be next. Your daddy's a coming for you. Whore."

"I've already seen him. Listen. I'm staying here in Nashville. For a little bit anyway. Have you seen dad?"

"Nope. Not yet. When I do, he'll be sorry."

"I love you, Fran. I'll take care of this real soon," I promised her, not knowing if I could.

"Make sure to feed Killer the senior dog food."

Holy Moley. I'd forgotten all about Gran's dog Killer. I let Gran go and called an Uber right away. Not even knowing where I was, I had to pinpoint my location on my cell to give an address. I started to wake Hallow but changed my mind. After all, the biker slept soundly, and I just didn't know anymore. All of a sudden, I had a bad feeling. Dad wasn't back in Arkansas, in all this time. Could I trust that Hallow or his club didn't run him down and kill him? Kingpin seemed keen on threatening the life of his innocent daughter, so I wouldn't put killing my dad past him. Part of me wanted to shake Hallow awake and demand answers. But, with this whole mess, I'd forgotten all about Killer. The old dog needed his medicine and to be let out of the house. With Gran gone, I was all he had now. I tried to think about how we left the door when Donette was shot. Had we shut it behind us? I hadn't been back to the house. Had the police officers searched the house? Poor Killer could be roaming the neighborhood. With all the farmland and wilderness, I'd never find him. I regretted coming to this cabin with Hallow more and more by the second.

Sadly, I had to put on Hallow's ex's clothes again. I'd take the Uber to the parking garage on Church Street and drive Gran's El Camino home to take care of Killer. There I could change and finally put on a bra. Then I'd have to drive back to Nashville and get to the police station to give them my statement. I had an entire day ahead of me before I could even wrap my head around what was going on with me and the biker. That was if he didn't let his club know about my dad's whereabouts. The big guy shuffled over to his side still sleeping as I tiptoed out.

HALLOW

Fucking hell. I'd slept in and couldn't find Eve anywhere. Her purse, and all evidence of her was long gone. Calling her, it went straight to her voicemail. Fuck. I went to text her but saw I had a voicemail from Thorn.

"Kingpin's looking for you. You missed church. He wants a report."

Fuck. I had missed Church. Saturday night I'd been here sound asleep with Eve.

A text from Pagan, our Vice President, sounded, telling me I better get my ass to Royal Road stat.

Fuck. I took my hog into Nashville, to the old industrial part of the city where you'd never know there was anything of any importance. There Royal Road hid amongst the abandoned warehouses. At the fence, I greeted my brother, Gunn, our day guard.

"They're looking for you," he said, right off.

"I've heard."

Inside, Kingpin sat at the bar, alone. Before I could join him, he said, "Fighting Cock was in my state, and you didn't tell me."

"Who said?" Fucking Thorn. I sat down at the bar with my President, a man I didn't know too well. He'd not chosen me to be a Royal Bastard, only took me in from another chapter. It was ten a.m. with not a soul to be found.

Kingpin poured me a drink and lit a joint. After a few tokes, letting me sweat, he said, "Villain heard from our spies in Arkansas that Fighting Cock was up in Nashville on Friday to get his daughter."

So, it hadn't been Thorn. I didn't know how much my President knew so I treaded carefully. I waited for him to go on.

Out of nowhere, Kingpin took the back of my head and slammed my face into the bar. Fuck. It stung like hell. My nose burned. Blood seeped into my mouth. I grabbed his shirt under his neck.

"Try me, pig," he warned.

As much as I wanted to bash his skull in, I let him go. Not that I couldn't take him, but I wasn't stupid. Challenge him, and I'd have the whole chapter on my ass in a New York minute.

Wiping at my nose, I said, "He didn't get her. Eve spent last night with me."

"Good. Where is she now?"

"She's home," I answered, thinking she'd probably gone on to her Gran's.

"She's ours now. I mean, yours. I put out the word that we claimed her as one of ours, unwillingly. Branded her. You're welcome."

"Won't that make the Gods mad? Stir up trouble."

Kingpin stared into the bottom of his glass. "Yes." He offered me the joint. I didn't usually, but with my nose about broke, I took a puff.

Kingpin slapped my back.

I flinched thinking he was going to hurt me again, and instantly felt like the biggest pussy.

"I want to see that tattoo, and she'll need to live with you, wherever you plan to be, upstairs or otherwise."

"About the cabin."

"Take it up with Cousin." Kingpin spoke of our club secretary who got the name from being related to most of the guys. I assumed Cousin took care of all the bookkeeping.

I moved to leave, thinking our conversation had ended. But I should have known better.

"Hallow. When you're done with her, she'll be one of our whores here. I hear she's a good singer. Maybe she needs a manager."

"Who says I'll be done with her?"

"You're a runner. You ran from your career when things got tough, running from the media, you ran from Charleston. I bet…"

"I'm not planning on leaving Royal Road or Eve."

"We'll see."

Goliath stepped behind the bar and about scared the shit out of me. Our other enforcer looked too much like Leviathan except he had hair and lacked the black tentacle

tattoos. Nonetheless, Goliath was scary enough. Bigger than shit, he was covered in colorful Japanese tattoos like he were a member of the Yakuza.

Kingpin waved him over but spoke to me. "Hallow, I want you to take on my man here, Goliath."

"What do you mean?" I asked him.

"I want you two to fight."

"When?" Goliath asked, cracking a grin.

"Friday," Kingpin replied, sealing my fate. He was punishing me, pitting me against one of his best fighters. I had no interest in getting in the cage, but we all did Kingpin's bidding. I'd flown under my President's radar so far, being Riff's whipping boy. Fighting this weekend would put a spotlight on me. Enormous Goliath fought like no one's business, was experienced. More than that, the stories about him chilled me to the bone. He gave the phrase cold blooded killer a whole new meaning. He'd been in the slammer with Kingpin. Where Kingpin had been an innocent man, Goliath was guilty of heinous crimes. He got out on a technicality. It'd been all Kingpin's doing. Witty fucker had found the loophole.

Speaking of wits, I spotted something metal and shiny behind the bar. "How about now?" I cracked my knuckles.

Goliath's face lit up.

"A private showing?" Kingpin was intrigued.

"Yes. Right here. Right now. I bet I can walk out of here in five minutes, unharmed."

Kingpin arched an eyebrow. "You know I'm a betting man. Sure. If you can walk out of here in five minutes, you won't have to fight on Friday." He glanced at his watch that was worth more than a million dollars. It'd been a gift from his famous brother. I'd never met a biker with such expensive tastes, but Royal Road's clientele were anything but poor. They had money to throw away hence the gambling that included betting on anything from our fights to world events. No matter the wager, Kingpin made sure Royal Road was always the true winner. All us members benefited. "Showtime." He spun on his stool and leaned back on the bar to watch.

Goliath jumped the bar. As I stepped back, amazed that the big guy was so nimble, he put up his fists. I dodged his first blow and went over the bar in the other direction. I grabbed the hand cuffs, I'd seen hanging. Memphis was one kinky bitch, so I was sure they were hers. Kingpin whipped around to watch me. When he spotted the shackles, he laughed. He knew my plans.

Goliath came at me, not leaping the counter but reaching over it to grab me. His meaty fingers touched my arm, but he couldn't catch me. I put one bracelet on his big wrist and hopped back over the bar. Behind him now, I jumped on his massive back. Wrapping my arm around his

fat neck, I put him in a choke hold, seized his other arm and cuffed his hands behind him, easy. My knee in his back, I got him on the ground, face first.

Goliath complained, "Fucking pig."

I bent down and whispered in his ear, "I'm not a cop anymore. I'm an outlaw. I can kill low lives like you anytime and no one can stop me."

My fist back, I planned to beat him to a bloody pulp, but Kingpin stopped me. "Fuck, brother." He clapped his hands. "I'm impressed. Go on and get out of here. Goliath, get up and get out of those cuffs."

As they searched for Memphis and her keys, I left to go find Eve.

On my way to Cottontown, I wondered why Eve left without telling me. I started to worry that she regretted our time together. That was unfortunate because she'd have to come live with me. She'd have to get my property patch etched into her perfect skin this week. We didn't have time for her to have any misgivings. I didn't look forward to fighting about it if it came to that. Regardless, I thought of how I would restrain her in case I couldn't reason with her. My dick got hard just thinking about it. I wondered how Eve would do in the basement at Royal Road.

Riding up to her house, I parked beside her porch. I found the door open and Eve sitting at her kitchen table on the phone. I started to ask her why she left. She held up her finger to quiet me.

"Okay, I'm coming to get him. Thanks for holding him." She got off the phone.

"What's going on?" I asked her.

"My Gran's dog, Killer. I have to go over and fetch him from old man Jennings's farm." Eve stood up and grabbed her car keys.

I followed her out the door, wanting to talk about why she left. She seemed solely focused on the dog. I stopped her. "Is that why you left? A dog?"

"Amongst other reasons, yes. I've got to move my things to Donette's place before the new owners get here."

"Eve, you'll have to come live with me. I mean, I want you to, too."

"Hallow, I don't even know if my dad is alive or if you had him killed." Her words stung.

"What? I wouldn't do that," I barked.

"Sure. I'm sure you bikers didn't tell someone my dad was in town," Eve hissed.

As we argued walking down the porch, I noticed a car stopping by Eve's mailbox. I hadn't thought anything of

it. It was broad daylight, after all. But suddenly, a man with a rifle appeared out of nowhere. On instinct, I rushed him, snatched his gun by the barrel and had it against his forehead in no time.

"What the actual fuck, man?" I asked him, Eve at my back.

Before he could answer, four others came up to the steps and joined him, three of them pointing guns at Eve and me. One man was dressed to the nines, wearing a full suit. The one lady looked mighty familiar.

"Viv?" Eve addressed her.

"From Bootsies?" I asked.

"Yeah." She winked at me. Viv waved her gun. "Let's go on inside shall we." They backed us through the door to the kitchen, but I never let go of the rifle. Eve clung to my back. Viv spoke to the man in a suit. "This is the girl."

He nodded, stuck his hands in his pockets, turned and walked out.

"What's going on?" I asked.

Viv laughed. "Wouldn't you like to know, detective?"

"She killed Grady," Eve announced.

Viv admitted to it. "Yes."

"I thought you questioned her?" Eve complained.

"I did." She'd been one of the Playboy Bunny bartenders I questioned. I'd tried to question them, but they'd been evasive. When I figured they were only coming on to me, I left them to join Eve. I asked Viv, "What's this about?"

"I'm tying up loose ends."

"But Ford?" Eve started.

"Ford never killed anyone except your slutty friend."

"Don't talk about Donette that way," Eve spat.

"You know she was sleeping with Grady, don't you?"

Eve's head went sideways.

"Grady was sleeping with everyone, including me. But that's not why I killed him."

"Then why did you?" I asked her point blank, pointing the rifle at her.

"I was just following orders." She glanced around. First at me holding the rifle and then at the others with their guns drawn on us. "Looks like you're outnumbered. Drop the rifle and I might let you live long enough to take Kingpin

a message from my boss." Viv puckered and smiled at the same time.

Doing the math, I steered the rifle down a hair.

Eve asked, "What about Earl?"

"I killed him, too, for alerting the Royal Bastards MC."

"But Jasper..." I started.

"Yeah, that poor boy did everyone's bidding. He killed your boy Sadist. What a shame. I liked him, Sadist that is. Not creepy Jasper."

"Who's orders?" I finally asked.

"Mr. Fond will not have Kingpin's men taking over Broadway. Tell him to quit recruiting his managers."

"All this killing for that?" Eve asked, her voice high.

"And one more," Viv said, her gun square on Eve who stepped out from behind my back. "I planned to pin it all on you, innocent Eve. That's what the text from Grady was all about. Oh, he typed all that out but was too scared to send it. He left it in his notes. I sent it and got in your locker to read it and reply."

"And you told the bikers about me, about my dad?"

"Yeah, I hoped they'd kill you so I wouldn't have to."

The whole time she confessed, I watched Viv's finger like a hawk. Therefore, I knew right when she was about to shoot. "Eve, run," I shouted, jumping in between Viv's gun and her chest. Somehow, I fired my rifle as Viv's bullet tore into my arm. I hit Viv in the leg, and she collapsed to the ground. Two of her goons were on me in a flash. One shot me in the thigh as the other tackled me. One of them ran after Eve who had run through the house. He brought Eve back into my view by the hair of her head.

"Why I ought to," the man began, taking down his pants.

Viv yelled out, "Give it to her good before we kill her. Boy's hold the biker's eyes open."

The man planned to rape Eve in front of me. I struggled as two men held me down, one shoving his fist into the wound in my leg. The other tried to go after my eyes. Viv held the hole in her leg and laughed like a cow. The man holding Eve had his dick out wrestling her around. She fell on the ground and began crawling away as he taunted her.

"Come get your last meal," he crooned

Helpless, I fought to get loose. With my good leg, I kicked one of the men in the chin while the man caught Eve by a leg and dragged her onto her back. As the worst was about to happen, I regretted ever knowing Eve. It was my fault she was in this mess. If I'd never gone to Bootsies on

Halloween, or didn't break up with Stephanie, none of this would be happening. Even so, I wouldn't close my eyes and let Eve suffer alone. As I watched the man, his pants around his ankles approach a very frightened Eve, the man's dick exploded. Blood squirted from his crotch as he stared down in horror. At the same time a shot had sounded, piercing my ears. Kingpin stepped into view, his shotgun visible to all. Out of nowhere Goliath tackled the men who secured me, both of them, removing them with ease.

"I ought to put you out of your misery," Kingpin said to Viv before he shot her other leg. "But I ain't gonna. You're going to prison with two bum legs. You'll be easy pickings. Tell Mr. Fond to eat my ass." Since I couldn't move, he helped Eve from the floor and started chatting with her like nothing had happened. "This your place?"

"It's my Gran's house." Eve rushed to me and sank to her knees. She tried to hold the blood in me. Blood was everywhere. Soon, Eve's hands were covered.

"And her name is?" Kingpin asked her. Eve answered him while she slapped at my face. My eyes had been closing, but she shook me awake.

"Hallow don't leave me. Don't shut your eyes."

Though weak, I obeyed her. I tried my best to keep them open.

Goliath easily maimed the rest of them, the guys that had been holding me, shooting them in the legs.

Kingpin picked up the landline and called the local police. "Four gunshot victims out at the Newberry place. Old lady shot here named Viv confessed to murdering Grady Foster Friday night."

My brothers had saved me from a fate worse than death, watching Eve be raped and killed. Grabbing Eve's keys, they got us into her car and out of there. Kingpin drove and Goliath followed on my President's unmistakable motorcycle. As he explained why he followed me out to Eve's, I thought about the man in a suit who'd left. Apparently, I asked Kingpin about him, though I forgot I had as soon as the words left my mouth.

"Mr. Noah Fond owns most of Nashville. You know, the devil wears a suit and tie."

I passed out after that. When I woke, I was in Heaven, Eve Angel smiling down at me. Like the angel she was, she sang.

CHAPTER 11

EVE

Hallow about bled out on the way to the hospital, especially since Kingpin decided to drive ninety miles per hour to Nashville, claiming he'd get better care. Following the other biker, he used the shoulder to avoid the traffic and about wrecked my Gran's car and killed us all. Meanwhile, this man who was so strong and virile knocked on death's door. Once Hallow was in the ER it was déjà vu. The doctor told us Hallow had to have emergency surgery on his leg and arm. He'd spend a couple of nights in the hospital. Kingpin placed a guard outside his room in the ICU so no one would mess with him. After what we'd just been through, I was thankful. But that guard wouldn't let me see him. I complained to Kingpin in the waiting room when he came from seeing Hallow.

"Why didn't you tell Payday you're Hallow's girl?"

I grumbled.

"They're taking him into surgery, anyhow. You should go wash up. The nurse has a change of clothes for you. Once he's out you can come with us and stay at Royal Road until he recovers."

"No way," I hissed.

Kingpin put his hands on me, on my arms and started rubbing as to sooth me. "Not that Royal Road, where you were on Halloween. Up in the Eagle's Nest. Ol' ladies can make a space for you for a few nights."

Not wanting him to touch me, I stepped away from him. "No thanks. I've got some loose ends to tie up," I said and thought of Viv saying that when she was trying to kill me. I decided to retire the phrase.

Then Kingpin insisted I come back to take care of Hallow when he gets out of the hospital. "It's the least you can do since he was saving your life," he said, when I wavered. "Actually, I saved your life. I say you owe me. Take care of my brother Hallow and we're square."

It's not that I didn't want to nurse Hallow back to health. I did. There was nothing in the world I wanted more. Hallow had just saved my life. Maybe Kingpin and the other biker, too. But more than that, I had lost too many people to lose Hallow, also, whether it be from him dying or just moving on. How did this stranger I met just a few days ago occupy so much of heart now? I ached to see him. I just didn't know if I felt safe at Royal Road after what had happened to me there.

"Maybe he can come to my place," I suggested to the head biker.

"I need him at Royal Road," Kingpin declared in a tone I couldn't argue with.

Reluctantly, I agreed with a bow.

Kingpin took that as an invitation to touch me again. His hands landed on my shoulders. "Since Hallow's out for the count, I have to warn you to keep quiet about Noah Fond. Tell anyone that he hired Viv to kill Wolf and you'll have a bigger target on your back than my club."

"I figured. And do I still have a target on my back?"

"Not as long as you're one of us."

I tried to tear loose of him, but Kingpin wouldn't let go. "If I'm Hallow's, why are you holding me?"

Kingpin released me. "I'm just teaching you a lesson, dear. Until you have a property patch, you're fair game. Be best if you learn our rules."

"Your rules?"

"Don't worry. If Hallow doesn't survive, I'll make a spot for you on the floor beside my throne. You belong to the Royal Bastards now with or without him."

Since I was covered in blood from bringing Hallow to the hospital, and I desperately wanted away from Kingpin, I took a shower in a bathroom the nurse showed me to. Once I was clean and dry, I put on a grey sweatsuit and non-skid socks. Seeing Hallow after his surgery about gutted me. Weak and groggy, he was barely awake, but he would survive, they said. After what had happened to Donette I didn't trust it. As it was, I wouldn't even lay on him. I didn't want to put any pressure on his chest. I kissed his head and held his hand for the longest time. He fell asleep, but I stayed. When the nurses left, I sang to him. I started humming several songs but settled into Norah Jones' "Come Away with Me". As the words flowed, I wanted nothing for Hallow to recover so we could be together. I thought of all the adventures we could have, together. I thought of sharing a long life with him, a future, but all I really wanted was to be in his arms again just one more time. I prayed for it, begging God not to take someone else from me.

When visiting hours were over, I went to Gran's to pack my things but stopped at Jennings's farm on the way. Thankfully, old man Jennings agreed to keep Killer. Good thing, because I didn't know if I could even have pets in Donette's apartment. The cops had cleared more dead bodies from Gran's property. This time with the action in the house, they'd left the crime scene tape all over. I was sure they wanted to talk to me. I hadn't even given them a statement about what happened to Donette, Ford and Jasper. I took another shower and put on my own clothes

for the first time in days. When I was about done packing, Donette's aunt called wanting to know if I would be at her wake this evening. After I packed my car, I dug out a black dress. Not only had I packed my belongings but most of Gran's as well since my brother had left the majority of her personal effects in the house. I drove to the funeral home with my car packed tight. I hugged everyone in Donette's family feeling a bit less to blame for my best friend's death now that I knew that the guy my dad hired to abduct me hadn't killed Grady. Ford had killed Donette, but I'd never know if he meant to. Maybe she'd only been in the crossfire. I'd have to ask Hallow's friend Thorn for clarity. Nevertheless, my best friend had been at Gran's in the first place thinking she was saving me.

I joined Celie in the corner. "I heard Viv went to jail for killing Grady," I said to her, my eyes red.

"Apparently, they were sleeping together."

"You know I wasn't sleeping with Grady, right?"

Celie never answered me, but said, "You've got a job if you want it."

"I'll think about it," I said to her, but knowing the man who owned Bootsies had my boss killed discouraged me.

Celie let me know Grady's funeral was right after Donette's tomorrow. She was joined by more crew from

Bootsies, and I slinked away, only to run into Dylan, Donette's ex.

"Eve," he started.

The sight of him shocked me. Donette had been a mess since he left her. Crying even harder, I left.

That night when I moved my things over to Donette's apartment, all her belongings were still there. Of course, her parents hadn't had the time to move them yet. I left everything just like she had it for the most part. From what I'd heard from Hallow, she'd had a guy over, that big biker Thorn the night she died. I went into her bedroom and made her bed and got rid of any evidence of Donette's wild sex life, so her mom didn't have to see it when she came over eventually to pack up. After all, what were best friends for? After boxing up lingerie and dildos, I locked myself in my new room. To my surprise, my brother texted me that my dad had made it home last night. I felt bad for suspecting Hallow would betray me. I didn't feel bad for thinking the other bikers might. I called the hospital to check on Hallow. The nurse told me that he was doing simply fine. I breathed a sigh of relief. Knowing dad was home and Hallow was alive, I slept pretty peacefully, considering.

Putting on the same black dress, I attended my best friend's funeral the next morning. I guess in Nashville funerals even had a live band. Jackie's Heroes were there, singing a sad, country "Purple Rain" that made me bawl my eyes out. I was too chicken shit to go up to the casket and

say goodbye, so I drove out to the cemetery afterwards for another chance. They opened her casket for the last time, and I finally made my way over. Reaching out, I touched her cold clammy hand.

"Donette, I miss you. I'm sorry for assuming you sold me out," I said to her in my mind. "Just so you know, Dylan showed up at the wake." I gave her a moment to process that. "And I took your advice and got laid. I promise to never take my time on this earth for granted again. I promise to get up and sing whenever I get the chance, for you, since I'm too chicken shit. I promise to love hard and fuck harder. I love you, girl."

Watching Donette placed in the ground, I ended up missing Grady's funeral all together. Probably for the best since everyone thought I'd been fucking the guy. No one had told me anything about Earl's funeral. Ford and Jasper, their deaths were tainted so I had no idea what was being done. I helped Donette's family take flowers and wreaths from the funeral back to their home in Antioch. I spent my time there refusing all the food people tried to feed me and in the arms of Donette's grandma whose soft skin and baby powder scent reminded me of my Gran. That night, I ate a bowl of cereal for dinner, while I flipped through my phone looking at pictures of me and Donette. When I was about to go to bed, Riff called me and said Hallow would be discharged in the morning.

"Kingpin said you'd be the one to take care of him. If you're not up to it, he said he's sure Memphis can nurse him."

"Memphis?"

"Blonde, big titties."

Oh, her. Thinking of another woman with Hallow, I barked, "I told Kingpin I'd be there."

Riff gave me directions to Royal Road. "After you get off the highway, go down the road until you hit Allan's Junk Cars, turn right right there and keep on going. After you go round Dead Man's curve, you're going to pass Sulfur Creek. Go on until you get down to the bridge down near the Pickin' Pickle Farm. You're going to take a left and take another left when you get to a trailer with no underpinning. Yonder down that road about five miles is where you're heading. Got it?"

"Got it," I said confidently.

"You're sure."

"Yes." I was from the south, after all.

"Hallow will be home after noon."

The next morning, I packed a suitcase not knowing how long I'd be taking care of Hallow. As I worried about if the bikers would get the doctor's instructions and pick up

any medicine he needed, I followed Riff's directions to a tee. When I got to the trailer without a stitch of grass in the yard surrounded by a lush forest, I knew I wasn't headed to Royal Road. That had been in the old industrial part of the city. Soon, I parked Gran's old El Camino in front of the cozy cabin Hallow took me to this weekend. At least I thought. There'd been about ten identical ones on the way. But at this one about twenty motorcycles were parked outside along with a few cars. At the top of the steep drive, the door was wide open. Walking inside I found Hallow in the front room surrounded by bikers and their women. A redheaded boy ran past my legs about knocking me down. A biker caught him and tossed him into the air.

"Oh, quiet down everyone. She's here," A woman announced, clapping her hands.

The crowd hushed and parted away from Hallow to let me through. Looking rough, he'd been propped up on the couch, one leg and one arm in casts. At the sight of him, I wanted to run to him and hug his thick neck. A flood of emotions about bowled me over. As it was, there was no room on the couch with him. A plump woman in leather pants with a nest of bleached blonde hair fed him chicken soup. Another older woman wearing a Black Sabbath t-shirt and cut offs patted the corner of his mouth with a napkin. She introduced herself as Allie then gave me a rundown of Hallow's care instructions.

The bikers I recognized and ones I didn't all continued shattering as the women asked Hallow, "Is this the girl going to be joining us here in the nest?"

"She is, though I haven't asked her yet. Not officially anyway," Hallow said to them.

"What are you talking about?" I asked.

Hallow's good arm pulled out a tiny velvet box. "Eve Angel Newberry, will you marry me?"

My hands flew up to my face to hide my shock. Everyone stared at me. I put my hands down. "Yes," I said instantly.

Allie had to open the box for him and handed him the ring. The older women moved so I could join him on the couch. With one hand, Hallow slid a small engagement ring on my finger. I barely looked at it because I could only look at him. Hallow's smile warmed my heart. Mainly, I was glad he was alive. In our awkward position, we kissed like no one was in the room. Like there was no tomorrow. Like life was way too short to wait for the right time. Or the right dick. Kissing Hallow, I had no regrets, no misgivings, nothing.

When our kiss ended, everyone cheered and clapped. A biker smashed his bottle of beer on the wooden floor. Allie complained she'd be cleaning that up. It'd been a set up. We were having an engagement party complete with cake and drinks. One of the bikers announced he'd be

grilling steaks out in the yard, so the crowd dispersed as people went outside. Allie, I liked her. I didn't have to ask, she just explained this whole neighborhood of cabins in the woods was part of Royal Road, the part the public didn't get to see. She called it the Eagle's Nest.

Riff told me, "In other words, we don't shit where we eat." Like that explained anything.

I saw Kingpin in the corner cozying up with a redheaded woman and thought about how Hallow told him we were together when we hadn't been. All to save me from their wrath. Still caught up in the moment, for the first time, I worried about whether this was real or not. It had all happened so fast. Beside Kingpin stood a huge man who looked meaner than a sack of wet cats. Bald with black tattoos of tentacles up his arms, on his head, he had to be Leviathan. He sure looked like he'd crash out of the ocean and kill me. He stared me down for a moment, his eyes dark and evil. I shivered, knowing he was the one wanting me dead. Kingpin snapped his fingers and the man walked away.

A biker came over with a tattoo gun. I turned to Hallow. "Hold on. I don't even know your real name." Saying it, I felt so stupid, but a brunette sat beside me and told me a story of how she met her husband, Dawg. She ended it telling me she hadn't known his real last name was Lingus.

"Why is that bad?"

"My name is Connie. So, of course, when we got hitched, I wanted to keep my last name. Dawg wouldn't have it. We went round and round. Well, Dawg surprised me. He officially changed his last name. So now, instead of Connie Lingus, I'm Connie Dawg."

Hallow chuckled, and it hurt him to do so. Coughing he said to me, "Don't worry. My last name ain't bad. It's August Adam Hart. Everyone called me Adam. It's just Hallow now."

What do you know, I'd found my Adam. Emotions took over, and I shed a happy tear. I never believed in fate. Losing my mom taught me early on bad things just happened to good people. After all the death this weekend, that was a truer fact than any. Finding Hallow meant good things just happened too.

Connie introduced me to a biker named Blitz who was apparently doing my tattoo right now on the couch. "Does it have to be on my neck?" I looked over to Kingpin as I asked, and his nose scrunched up as he shook his head. I picked my upper thigh. It'd show if I wore my daisy dukes, but I didn't mind it. One of the women gave me a pair of shorts to change into. I disappeared to the bathroom to change, not the one in the bedroom, but one right off the living room. Washing my hands, I stared at the ring on my finger. My nerves threatened to ruin things for me. I wanted to run out the front door, but then I remembered about Donette. She was dead and gone. She'd told me a million

times to not wait to start living. I thought about how I felt when I felt I might lose Hallow too. I wanted to experience life with him. Walking out of the bathroom I felt resolved and happy about saying yes. However, I bumped into the fuchsia haired woman from the night I met Hallow, Steph.

"Hallow's only marrying you cause Leviathan said he had to," she said with a smirk.

Before I could say a word, she vanished into the bathroom.

I wandered back to join Hallow on the couch with a million misgivings. Hallow wasn't all there. He was on painkillers from the surgery. Allie explained that they were just now kicking in. "I gave him one right before you got here. He'd been waiting a while. He wanted to be coherent to ask you."

My man laid back beside me on the couch, all mangled, all because he tried to save me. I wasn't about to cause a scene and ask if what his ex said was true, but Steph's words still haunted me. A biker I hadn't met poured me a shot of whiskey to help with the pain of the tattoo. I downed it. Another biker sat up on the table in the little dining area with a guitar and started strumming a tune. It was Nashville after all. A woman got up to sing, "To Make You Feel My Love".

Hallow, as drowsy as he was, took my hand in his good one and kissed it. He whispered against my skin, "I picked this one for you. I heard you singing to me in the hospital. That settled it, but hell even before then, I knew I'd never want to lose you, Eve Angel."

At his sweet words and listening to the stunning lyrics he'd dedicated to me, I had no more question that Hallow loved me. I felt his love through and through. We'd not even told each other we loved each other. We hadn't needed to. I decided to never think about what Steph said again.

Dimple took over after the song ended, singing, "Burning Love" as only Elvis could. It was a recipe for an instant party.

Hallow was out of it. He asked, "Is this song for me."

I chuckled. "Yes, you're my hunk of burning love."

I jumped when the tattoo gun touched me. Hallow squeezed my hand. "Don't be afraid. I won't let you fall," he whispered.

"Fall?" I asked. Hallow was falling asleep.

"I won't let you fall off the bull."

Laughing again, I patted his hand. "I know you won't."

Beside a very sleepy Hallow, I got tattooed right in front of a cabin full of bikers and their women, their kids.

Whiskey flowed. People danced. Even Steph looked on. Leviathan, I didn't see him again. With the music playing and atmosphere much like Bootsies, without the groping and me having to serve people, I relaxed. Blitz simply tattooed, "Property of Hallow, Royal Bastards MC, Nashville, TN," in a bold, fancy font on my thigh, but it meant the world to me. All the while I wolfed down a piece of chocolate cake.

By the time Blitz finished my tattoo, Hallow was asleep. He'd see his property patch later. I had no idea where our road headed, but I was no longer afraid, not with him by my side.

The End For Now

For all the songs that played in this novel visit Hallow Eve's Playlist on Spotify
Enjoyed this story? Be sure to leave a review!

To read all about Hallow and Eve's wedding make sure to pick up the next installment,
Royal Road
Royal Bastards MC: Nashville, TN Chapter

Beau Strick aka Kingpin, President of the Royal Bastards MC in Nashville, Tennessee has never let his twin brother, Country Music star Beau Strick's use of his real name bother him. After all, he'd hate to be the one named

Bubba. The fact most of his brother's hit songs are actually the soundtrack to his tragic life never truly fazed him either until he saw Maddy Mae on his brother's arm.

Word travels fast in these parts. As soon as Maddy Mae moves home to Music City, she has a call from her high school sweetheart. She thinks twice about answering. Sure, she knows he's famous now. He could finally be her ticket to success as a songwriter, but her heart shattered long ago when Beau went to prison. That heartache's something she never wants to experience again.

Meeting up with his brother Bubba seems innocent enough until she finds herself falling for his persona. However, Bubba's like loving Beau without any of the baggage.

Why did they ever head down Royal Road?

Nashvegas is full of honky-tonks but none as infamous as Royal Road where the Royal Bastards MC rule. Confronted with her old flame, the real Beau Strick and all his demons, Maddy's torn between two identical brothers. Well, they used to be identical. Now, the real Beau looks nothing like the clean-cut Country Music star who sings about his hard knocks. Kingpin's long hair and tattoos, the rev of his Harley calls to something wild within her.

Maddy Mae is the one thing about Kingpin that hasn't changed. His love for her is the last thing left of his soul. And she's the only thing he won't let his brother take from him. His twin has plenty of money and influence in Music City, but Kingpin controls its underbelly, not to mention an army of outlaws on Harleys. He'll go to war if he must. Whether Maddy Mae agrees doesn't matter. Kingpin will convince her there's nothing better than the real thing.

For the continuation of this series, sign up for news
http://www.morganjanemitchell.com/join

www.morganjanemitchell.com
For ARC and signed paperbacks & more
Join
Morgan Jane's Facebook Group

ABOUT THE AUTHOR

Award winning, USA Today Bestselling Author Morgan Jane Mitchell spent years blogging politics and health trends before she rediscovered her love of writing fiction. Trading politicians for bloodsuckers of another kind, she's now the author of bestselling post-apocalyptic fantasy novel, Sanguis City. Her action-packed series of vampires, witches, demons and zombies is paranormal romance, dystopia, urban fantasy and erotica in one bite. When Morgan Jane is not creating the city of blood or conjuring up other supernatural tales, she's dreaming up erotic and dark romances including her latest bestselling erotic suspense, Asphalt Gods' MC series.

JOIN MY NEWSLETTER
http://www.morganjanemitchell.com/join

LIKE MORGAN JANE MITCHELL
on Facebook

JOIN MORGAN JANE'S FACEBOOK GROUP
#teammorganjane
Bookbub
Books2Read
Instagram
Twitter

READ MORE FROM
MORGAN JANE MITCHELL

READING ORDER

Asphalt Gods' MC

SCAR

Seven Sunsets

Hell on Heelz (standalone)

Sunrise

Cowboy, Take Me

Picking Bones

Lucky Stars

Bone Daddy

Mud

Trax

Snakebite

Hawk

Freedom

Slayer (standalone)

Asphalt Gods' MC Series

Scar, Asphalt Gods MC

Emery wants to die. Good thing she just ran into a killer. *"They say what doesn't kill you makes you stronger, but that's bullshit. What doesn't kill you leaves a scar. More than the eyesore down my torso, I was a scar, the jagged, fucked up remains of a tragedy."*

Scar's Nomad status gives him a chance to fulfill his one wish, but his lonely mission is interrupted when a possible one-night stand goes horribly wrong.

"They say what doesn't kill you makes you stronger, but what if I can't live with myself anymore?"

Finding the blonde face down in a puddle of her own blood jeopardizes everything. Saving her and keeping her quiet could get Scar killed, but when Emery wakes up, her shocking proposal for him to kill her starts the ride of his life.

Hell on Heelz, an Asphalt Gods' MC novel

Morgan Jane Mitchell An Asphalt Gods' MC Novel. Full length, Stand Alone.

"They say time heals all wounds, but my time's done run out. I'm no spring chicken, but it's more than that. I've been mad as hell for far too long. It's made me a different woman, a bitter woman. No, they don't call me Rage for nothing—I'm a twisting bitch tornado and that's before you make me mad. When I'm not fuming, I'm secretly festering in suffocating smog of self-loathing. A man did this to me, and now that I've finally met another man, one who calms my storm, one I might let break through the thick thorny vines I've wrapped around my heart—I fear there's nothing left of me."

Edie Pearl better known as RAGE never thought her decision to leave her cheating husband and join the Hell on Heelz would land her as the potential President of the female outlaw motorcycle club when the Banshee is killed. Rage has spent the last two years mad as hell, nursing her broken heart with booze and fast men. When she's pitted against her fellow heel, Dixie, in a race to track down the Banshee's killer, she meets the man of her dreams. Mud may be the only man to get her motor running, but he's also her sworn enemy. Will Rage do the unthinkable and choose a man over her club? Or is time really up for her?

Mud's been a mess since his twin brother left the Asphalt Gods' MC. He'd hate to have to kill his own kin. When Scar shows Mud mercy by sparing his brother, he thinks everything will finally be back to normal. He's proven wrong. A ride to California is interrupted with by the Heelz. After he leaves his brothers and catches up to his enemy, he finds a beautiful woman, one he cannot resist. Him showing her the same mercy puts him in even more jeopardy. His heart on the line with his life, which road will he choose?

Cowboy, Take Me, Asphalt Gods' MC
Morgan Jane Mitchell

"I've been waiting all my life for a Cowboy." When Cowboy finds Halley outside of the Devil's Den, it's a damned dream come true for her, but she's not alright. With all the double-crossing going down within the Gods, Cowboy hides Scar's sister away until she's well and he can get a hold of Scar. He never expected to fall in love. When the two arrive in Tucson, they aren't alone, and Scar is beside himself.

Picking Bones, Asphalt Gods' MC
Morgan Jane Mitchell

"Suzi was a bone. Like when I hunted one, a piece of my enemy, a substitute would not do... Nothing could satisfy me until I had her again..."

Can a one-night stand lead to a lifetime of love?

Bones heads to California not only to help Cowboy rescue the woman he loves, he's left something in Texas. Suzi has something that belongs to him. Not his heart. His unborn child means more to him than she can ever know.

Her life finally on track, Suzi doesn't want a thing to do with an outlaw, let alone to raise her baby around one.

Bones, not used to hearing no, does the unimaginable. At least Suzi couldn't imagine being kidnapped and hauled back to Louisiana, especially in her condition.

When they're done picking bones, will Suzi pick Bones?

Bestselling Erotic Romance Table 21 Series In Too Deep (Table 21, Book #1) Morgan Jane Mitchell

25-year-old Loraine Wynters has always been in control. She takes what she wants, from a new man every night -and leaves. Too bad this has cost her last job and landed her in the local sex addict's support group where she is certain she doesn't belong. Within this group of weirdos, she sees a familiar face. Richard Mahoney may be the gorgeous 30-year-old, successful owner of Table 21, but he has lost more than Loraine could ever imagine because of his obsession. After learning all her secrets, Loraine's new boss Rick is determined to fix her with his own brand of therapy. After digging deeper, Loraine finds that her boss needs more than just physical healing. Can they repair each other so they can be with other people?

With both Loraine and Rick longing for a normal life, will a pact between them be the answer to both their problems? Or are they getting in too deep?

Bestselling Paranormal Romance, Sanguis City Series Morgan Jane Mitchell

Ever wonder what happens *after* the world ends?

Lilanoir Rue did. A mere by product of the destruction, she never knew what had happened before hand either. Banished from the only place she called home, the Human Reservation, she wipes her tears and never looks back.

In a world gone dead, life has never been so good, for some. While others live in chaos, the chosen call Sanguis City home. The rich and powerful found a way to survive The End and to enjoy every minute of it, for eternity. On the brink of a gruesome death from starvation, disease or a hungry mutant, humans flock to sell their blood for peace.

The city of blood, made for and by vampires welcomes Noir, her kind are in high demand. Neither Human nor Vampire, Bleeders take care of the city in

the daylight. Draining humans by day and dating Vampires at night leaves Noir little time to think about her past, or much else, until it finds her.

ROYAL BASTARDS MC SERIES
THIRD RUN

Winter Travers: Monk

K.L. Ramsey: Ratchet's Revenge

Chelle C . Craze & Eli Abbott: Cocked Hammer

Nikki Landis: Hell's Fury

M. Merin: Diesel

Kristine Allen: Chains

KE Osborn: Seeking Shadows

Scarlett Black: River

Erin Trejo: Bleed for Me

Crimson Syn:Afflicted with Desire

J.Lynn Lombard: Torch's Torment

Glenna Maynard: Taken by the Biker

K Webster: Dragon

Khloe Wren: Flood of Bravery

Rae B. Lake: Chaos and Paradise

Misty Walker: Bexley's Biker

J.L. Leslie: Worth the Pain

Nicole James: Climbing the Ranks

Ker Dukey: Carnage

Deja Voss: Steel Resurrection

Elle Boon: Royally Inked

Jessica Ames: Into the Flames

Shannon Youngblood: Sex and Candy

B.B. Blaque: Southern Ballz

K.L. Savage: Raven

Izzy Sweet & Sean Moriarty: Broken Lines

E.C. Land: Spiral into Chaos

Jax Hart:Desert Heat

Royal Bastards MC Facebook Group -
https://www.facebook.com/groups/royalbastardsmc/
Website- https://www.royalbastardsmc.com/

Made in the USA
Monee, IL
23 July 2025

21501271R00128